Thou Shalt Not Dump the Skater Dude

and other commandments I have broken

Thou Shalt Not Dump the Skater Dude

And Other Commandments I Have Broken

By

Rosemary Graham

VIKING

VIKING
Published by Penguin Group
Penguin Young Readers Group, 345 Hudson Street, New York, New York 10014, U.S.A.
Penguin Group (Canada), 90 Eglinton Avenue East, Suite 700, Toronto, Ontario, Canada M4P 2Y3 (a division of Pearson Penguin Canada Inc.)
Penguin Books Ltd, 80 Strand, London WC2R 0RL, England
Penguin Ireland, 25 St Stephen's Green, Dublin 2, Ireland (a division of Penguin Books Ltd)
Penguin Group (Australia), 250 Camberwell Road, Camberwell, Victoria 3124, Australia (a division of Pearson Australia Group Pty Ltd)
Penguin Books India Pvt Ltd, 11 Community Centre, Panchsheel Park, New Delhi – 110 017, India
Penguin Group (NZ), Cnr Airborne and Rosedale Roads, Albany, Auckland 1310, New Zealand (a division of Pearson New Zealand Ltd)
Penguin Books (South Africa) (Pty) Ltd, 24 Sturdee Avenue, Rosebank, Johannesburg 2196, South Africa

Penguin Books Ltd, Registered Offices: 80 Strand, London WC2R 0RL, England

First published in 2005 by Viking, a division of Penguin Young Readers Group

1 3 5 7 9 10 8 6 4 2

LIBRARY OF CONGRESS CATALOGING-IN-PUBLICATION DATA
Graham, Rosemary.
Thou shalt not dump the skater dude and other commandments I have broken / by Rosemary Graham.
p. cm.
Summary: Having endured the vicious rumors spread by her ex-boyfriend, a professional skateboarder, high school sophomore Kelsey Wilcox tries to salvage her reputation while attempting to earn a place on her high school newspaper.
ISBN 0-670-06017-8
[1. Gossip—Fiction. 2. Skateboarders—Fiction. 3. Journalists—Fiction. 4. Self-confidence—Fiction. 5. High schools—Fiction. 6. Schools—Fiction. 7. Berkeley (Calif.)—Fiction.] I. Title.
PZ7.G7558Tho 2005 [Fic]—dc22 2005003928

Printed in U.S.A
Set in Sabon
Book design by Nancy Brennan

For my Father,
James F. Graham

× × ×

It took a while to figure
this one out. Big thanks to Joy
Peskin, whose wise counsel finally set
this book on course; to Leigh Feldman, for
her continued support; and to Laura Ruby and
Lesley Quinn for cheerfully reading every draft I
put before them. The Saint Mary's College Faculty
Development Fund supported this project. The
Hidden Valley Artists Retreat Center provided a
beautiful place to write. Kevin Griffin and
Graham Lillian Griffin provided the
love, encouragement, and patience
that kept me going.

PART
xxx
ONE

1

When Parents Make Drastic, Life-Altering Decisions

I know it's a cliché, and English teachers say we're not supposed to use them, but my life has pretty much been a roller-coaster ride for the last three years.

It started when my mom gave me and my brother, Josh, all of two months' notice that we were moving away from Boston, the place I'd called home my entire life. She had just turned thirty-five. Her and Dad's divorce was finally finalized and now, she said, it was *her* time to pursue *her* dreams.

And guess what?

Her dream was to go to law school.

And guess where?

Oh, in Berkeley, California, a.k.a. three thousand miles away.

× × ×

Okay. Let me just say that if you're going to move across the country and change schools and friends and all that stuff, I strongly recommend that you do it either right before the middle-school years, or just after them—not, as I did, right at the beginning of eighth grade.

If one or both of your parents decides it's necessary for their career, as in my case, or that it's in the family's best interest—or something like that—you must do all you can to stop the plan: Beg. Cry. Sigh. A lot. If necessary, refuse to eat your favorite dessert.

(But don't go all anorexic. You don't want to end up in some psych ward, with nurses measuring your every mouthful and a roommate itching to get a finger down her throat.)

If none of the above work, tell your parents this: Experts say it's better for moves to coincide with natural transitions and milestones in a child's life—like the summer between middle school and high school.

This is actually true. I researched it, using sources my grandmother—who's a therapist—recommended. Of course, my mom just rolled her eyes when I made my presentation—with PowerPoint graphs—but it might work for you.

Believe me, you do not want to be the new girl in

eighth grade. You especially do not want to be the new girl at a private, girls-only middle school.

Your efforts will probably be in vain, as mine were, because usually when parents make drastic, life-altering decisions, they believe they have good reasons. And I can see how, from my mother's point of view, moving from Boston to Berkeley at the beginning of my eighth-grade year was the right thing to do.

For her.

See, she got accepted at Boalt Hall, the University of California's ultra-competitive law school. She got in a few other places, too, but Boalt was the best name brand, which in my family, especially where schools are concerned, is very important. Plus, my mom's parents live in Berkeley, in a huge house with enough rooms for all of us to have one of our own.

Oh, sure, she figured I'd have some adjusting to do, but she said I'd always made friends easily.

"Maybe a little too easily," she actually said. "It'll be good for you to find your way in a new social landscape." Ever since deciding to go back to school, my mother had been throwing around phrases like "social landscape," "economic disparity," and "political framework."

Dad, who's "still very much a part of this family"—

according to him and Mom and their divorce consultant, Stan—was totally behind Mom's going to Boalt, and totally opposed to my staying behind with him.

"It'll never work, Kels. I'm on the road three out of five nights a week."

He promised we'd see him plenty since his company was expanding into Northern California. He said he might even buy a place out here himself and become "bi," as in "bicoastal," which he actually thinks is funny.

× × ×

As the reality of the move began to sink in and my efforts at persuasion failed, I got desperate. And in my desperation, I learned something about myself.

But this wasn't a good, get-to-know-yourself-better-and-you'll-grow kind of thing. It was a previously unknown, totally mind-blowing biographical fact.

Here's how it came up: Mom and I were sitting at the kitchen table, laptop to laptop. I was supposed to be writing an essay about why I thought the Susan B. Anthony Academy for Girls was a good educational choice for me. Mom was filling out the parents' forms. Susan B. Anthony was a new middle school started by a friend of my grandmother's, founded on the idea that the sixth-, seventh-, and eighth-grade years are "a girl's most challenging time, when her social and intellectual blabeddy blah were blabeddy blabeddy blabeddy blah."

According to my grandmother, there was "a waiting list a mile long," and her friend Arlene was doing us a huge favor by offering me the one unexpected opening in the eighth-grade class.

Mom said she thought a small all-girls' school would help "cushion my landing" in California. (Yes, this is the same woman who just weeks prior to this statement suggested I'd had it too easy in the friend department.)

I didn't really care about the all-girls part. Let's face it: Eighth grade is not a peak year for the male species. All I knew was I didn't want to change schools at all.

I had just slept over at my friend Calina's house. We had stayed up practically all night, watching movies and spying on her older brother and his friends shooting baskets in their driveway. Of course I knew that high-school boys shot baskets in driveways all over the country, but I wanted to watch *these* boys. One in particular. I'd had my eye on Calina's brother's friend Marc for two years, and he was just starting to notice me. You should have seen how he smiled when he said "Hey" to me the night before. Now my mother was going to tear me away from this very promising situation.

I tapped away on my keyboard and read aloud. "The Susan B. Anthony Academy for Girls is a good educational choice for me because . . ."

Mom ignored me.

"Because I have no other choice in the matter. I am being torn away from the only school I have ever known, from all the people I call friends, and dragged three thousand miles so my mother can pursue her dreams at my expense."

That got her attention. I looked up and found myself the object of The Stare. The unblinking, guilt-inducing look that says, *I am so disappointed/disgusted by what you said/did that I cannot begin to find words.*

Only this time, after holding The Stare for an eternity, and taking an extra-long, extra-deep breath, my mother found words all right.

"You know, Kelsey, I sacrificed a lot for you. Can't you just suck it up?"

And then, before I could even open my mouth to offer a halfhearted "Sorry," my mother proceeded to tell me—for the first time in my life—that she and

Dad had gotten married when they did because she was pregnant.

With me.

"Oh, we were going to get married anyway. Don't be so dramatic. You are not the *reason* we got married. But getting pregnant when I did meant I had to put my law-school plans on hold. Your father was just starting his business."

He's in commercial real estate, by the way.

"And back then, we hardly had rent money, never mind money for child care."

We have a lot more now, by the way.

"Plus I didn't want to hand you off to someone and go sit in a lecture hall. So I withdrew my applications."

That was so unfair. Like I *asked* her to postpone her career?

For about two days after Mom dropped that bomb, I walked around thinking about all the what-ifs the news raised in my head.

What if she hadn't gotten pregnant then? Would they have gotten married at all?

What if she had gone to law school at the normal law-school age and waited to have kids? Would my parents have had a happier marriage?

Maybe if Mom had had a career earlier on, she

wouldn't have gotten all fed up being the wife of the self-made, rags-to-riches businessman known as my dad. And maybe . . .

But after two days I realized that everyone in the world could ask an unending series of what-if questions about their own conception. I mean, aren't we all just random products of that one egg whose month has finally come and that one particular sperm that survives its journey?

Which is another reason I decided to stop asking "What if?"

Pondering the particulars of your parents' sex life is not a healthy way for a girl to spend her daydreaming moments.

2

A Supportive Atmosphere of Friends

From the mission statement of the
Susan B. Anthony Academy for Girls:

The small, girls-only approach allows for truly
individualized learning in an intimate,
supportive atmosphere of friends.

Switching schools at the beginning of eighth grade turned out to be worse than I'd imagined. Way worse.

Susan B. Anthony is tiny. As in twenty-students-per-grade tiny.

And that "supportive atmosphere of friends" stuff?

Right.

I'd never really known just how tight cliques could be until I came to SBA and found myself on the outside for a change. The eighth grade was ruled by two girls, Melinda and Mallory, who had a hypnotic hold on the rest of the girls in the class. Even the girls who were not a part of the inner M&M circle—as they actually called themselves—were somehow controlled by them. Neither M was nice, or smart, judging from the 74 and 69 I happened to see when the semester's first algebra test was passed back. (I got a 91, which kind of surprised me. But I guess that's what happens when you don't have any friends—you pay attention in class and have more time for studying at night.) But still, they ruled.

Okay, even though I don't have the most sophisticated vocabulary, here's a big word I can use correctly: impenetrable. As in, the social circles, a.k.a., cliques, at SBA are impenetrable. Actually, Mim—that's my-grandmother-the-therapist, whose real name is Myra—came up with "impenetrable" when I broke down and told her about how miserable I was at Anthony after one particularly humiliating day.

I had walked to the cafeteria with Serena Carter, who was part of the M&M circle. She was being really nice and friendly and asking me all about my old school and how I liked living in California and telling me about how her grandparents lived in

Massachusetts. She kept talking to me and asking me questions as we went through the food line. After we paid for our lunches, I kept walking with her, thinking we were going to sit down together. But when we got to the table where Melinda and Mallory and company always ate, there was just one empty chair and Serena put her tray down in front of it. Then she turned to me and said, "Nice talking to you."

The thing is, there was definitely room at the table for another chair, and the table next to it had three empty ones. But no one said, "Sit down with us," or, "Hey, let's make room for Kelsey, the newest member of the SBA family," or, "Pull up a chair."

They just looked at me, like they were waiting for me to go away.

Which I did.

"Oh, yeah, nice talking to you, too," I said, trying to sound like I had someplace else to go. And I walked away and kept walking straight ahead until I had to either sit down or take my tray out into the hall, which wasn't allowed, and so I plopped myself in the first empty chair I saw and found myself surrounded by sixth-graders playing a game they called Green Jell-O Gross-Out.

Under different circumstances, I too might have cracked up to the point of almost peeing my pants at the sight of Mindy Alswanger with two thin strips of the stuff hanging out of her nostrils, saying, with a totally straight face, "Does anyone have a tissue?" But sitting among the happy, laughing sixth-graders—who hadn't yet divided themselves into the strict cliques of the seventh- and eighth-graders—just made me feel worse.

Somehow, I managed to hold it together through that afternoon's humanities seminar, "Women in Art: More than Models," but as soon as three o'clock rolled around and I could finally escape into the shelter of Mim's old Volvo, I cried. These weren't the won't-you-feel-sorry-for-me-and-postpone-your-law-school-plans-for-one-more-year tears I'd been squeezing out for the months before our move. These were genuine I-have-no-friends-and-nobody-likes-me-for-no-good-reason tears.

Tears of injustice.

Tears of rage.

"Do you want me to call Arlene?" Mim asked, after I'd managed to choke out the story.

"No! Do not call Mrs. Myerson. Start the car, Mim. Get me out of here." Some of the sixth-grade girls from lunch were walking by, peering into Mim's car and waving, smiling their big, shiny, braces-filled smiles at their new friend, Kelsey the Eighth-Grade Outcast.

As grandmothers go, Mim is pretty cool. She is a therapist after all, so she really does understand a lot about why people act how they do.

But sometimes, she's more than a little out of touch. As if she could call her friend Arlene and *poof!* I'd have friends.

3

WHAT'S ON THE INSIDE

While there was nothing Mim could do about the friend situation at SBA, she did indirectly help me make my first and to this day best friend in Berkeley.

Amy and I probably never would have become friends if it hadn't been for our grandmothers being best friends and our getting thrown together for Sunday night dinners and other family gatherings a bunch of times during my first few months in Berkeley.

On the surface, we're very different. Amy's a Punky Retro Goth Vegan with Straight-Edge tendencies. That means no drugs, tobacco, or alcohol, and no animal products "in your mouth or on any other part of your body." She dyes her hair a different color practically every week and never wears anything—except underwear—that isn't used and isn't authentically late seventies/early eighties.

I would never wear anything used unless I knew the previous owner really, really well. Like my mom. Maybe. I would never even think about dyeing my hair, which is one of my best features. (My mom's stylist tells me it takes three hours in foils and costs two hundred bucks to get anywhere close to my shade of blonde.) Cigarettes? Yeah, they're totally gross. And while I don't see a lot of substance abuse in my future, no way would I sign on for the Straight-Edge abstinence plan at such a young age. Besides, I love the little half-glasses of champagne I get when my parents or grandparents are toasting something.

So if Amy and I had met under normal teenage circumstances, we probably would have made all those assumptions and judgments based on appearance that teenagers know we're not supposed to make because *it's what's on the inside that counts* but of course we make anyway.

x x x

Amy was the only one who believed me that Susan B. Anthony wasn't exactly the hotbed of peace, love, and understanding it claimed to be.

"Do you know how much it costs to go to that

Girl Power school?" she asked me one Saturday when we were browsing at a vintage shop on Telegraph Avenue.

I shook my head. My parents never discussed the prices of things with me. My dad said he'd spent his whole childhood worrying about money and he didn't want his kids to grow up worrying about it. As a result, I'd grown up the opposite of worried. I was pretty oblivious to what things cost.

"Try nineteen thousand dollars a year." Amy pulled a red satin slip-negligee thingy off the rack and held the hanger under my chin. "You should really try this on."

I pushed it away. "Uck. You're not serious."

"About the dress, or the nineteen thou?"

"Both." I wasn't entirely clueless: I knew school tuition was in the thousands. But if I'd had to guess, I would have guessed half of that amount, tops.

Amy walked over to the mirror and held the negligee under her own chin. But her hair was green that week and the effect was, well, Christmas-y. She scrunched her nose at her reflection.

"Maybe with a different color hair?" I offered.

"Nah," she said. "This is sixties, anyway." She placed it back on the rack.

"Hey Sal." Amy was on a first-name basis with all the vintage clothing dealers in Berkeley.

Sal, who wore a beautiful blue silk dress with a cinched waist, black fishnet stockings, black pumps, and a matching blue pillbox hat, looked up from the computer. "Yeah?" Her lipstick was the reddest I've ever seen.

"What d'you have that's late seventies?"

Sal shook her head. "Nothing you haven't seen. Sorry. I've got a shipment coming in on . . . wait a sec—" She clicked her mouse and studied her computer monitor. "Friday. If I see anything that looks like your style, I'll put it aside."

"That would be great. Thanks. And remember . . ."

"No leather," said Sal with a smile. "You got first dibs on the vinyl, honey."

× × ×

"Nineteen thousand dollars?" I said, as we stepped over the legs of a couple of kids sprawled on the sidewalk outside of Sal's.

I guess I said it kind of loud, because one of the kids we stepped over whistled and said, "Nineteen thousand dollars? You ladies are talking some high finance there."

It was hard to say how old he was. He had facial hair—a short but raggedy beard with a little braided and beaded tail coming off the chin. But if you shaved all that off (which would have been the first thing I'd do if I was in charge of his makeover), you might find a sixteen- or seventeen-year-old underneath.

"How's about contributing one little old dollar for our food fund?" He nodded at a couple of scruffy guys sitting against the wall playing cards. One was wearing a spiked dog collar and a torn Winnie-the-Pooh T-shirt, the other a beat-up leather jacket over his bare, very pale chest. "Me and my buddies are hoping to have enough for half-price pizza night tonight."

The buddies gave us a stoned "hey" and went back to their game.

"Sorry," I said with a shrug and an apologetic smile. We were just coming up to ShoeTique, one of my favorite stores. I stepped up to the display window and watched in the reflection as Amy stopped to talk to the guys. She dug a crumpled bill out of the front pocket of her jeans and held it out to the one with the beard scraggle, smiling and talking the whole time. He took it and jammed it into his own front pocket. I was too far away to hear what they were saying, but from the looks of it, he was introducing his friends. The one with the dog collar gave Amy a little salute, and the pale-chested one held out a gimme-some fist. Amy leaned over and gave him some. Then the guy she'd given the dollar to pointed at me and Amy looked toward me and shrugged. I ducked into the store.

It's always been my family's policy not to give money to people on the street.

The only time I ever saw my dad violate the policy was one winter in Boston when I was around eight. He had Josh and me by the hand and we were walking in the snow to meet Mom somewhere. We passed a mother with two little kids—like two-and-three little—sitting outside a subway stop. At first, he'd just given his usual, "Nope, sorry," and kept walking. But then he looked at me and Josh, and looked back over his shoulder at the woman, who kept saying, "Spare any change? Spare any change?" to the people walking by. Dad dug into his pocket, peeled three twenties off his money clip, rolled them around each other, and stomped back to the woman while Josh and I watched.

I remember the amount because I was just learning multiplication, and I was proud of myself for being able to figure out that three times twenty was sixty and proud of my dad for giving sixty whole dollars to a woman who had been asking only for change.

Dad placed the twenties on the woman's gloved palm and folded her fingers over them. She gasped. And then started crying and shouting, "God bless you, sir! God bless you!"

I remember also that I didn't understand why Dad seemed so embarrassed and also mad at the time. People were staring at him and the weeping woman, who actually got down on her knees, like they weren't sure if maybe he was hurting her and maybe they should do something about it.

Dad lowered his voice to an almost-whisper and said, "Don't thank me. Don't thank me." Holding her by the elbow, he helped her to her feet. "Just take care of those kids, okay? Get them something hot to eat." Then he grabbed me and Josh by our hands and pulled us down the sidewalk like he couldn't get away fast enough.

I hadn't seen him give a single penny to anyone since that day.

But he gives money—a lot of money, he told me when I asked him a few years later why he didn't "help people" on the street anymore—to a program that provides shelter and job training for single mothers and their kids.

"Giving a dollar here or a dollar there doesn't really do anything, honey."

"But remember the time you gave that lady sixty dollars? I bet that really helped her," I said. This was back when I still thought sixty dollars was a lot of money.

He smiled and shrugged. "Yeah, maybe. Mostly, I think it helped her to think that someone cared. I give my money to a place that really knows how to help people like that lady."

Now that I'm older, I understand it more. Like Dad says, it doesn't make "fiscal sense" to give away little amounts to individuals on the street. Better to make donations to organizations that know how to help the people help themselves. Maybe I'd talk to him about finding a youth program to donate to. Mim probably knew someone. Mim always knows someone or knows someone who knows someone.

But to be honest, it wasn't just the family policy that kept me from giving money. The street kids scared me. And as long as I'm being completely honest, I may as well admit that they pissed me off, too.

Just a few weeks before, when I was on my way

to the law library to meet my mom for lunch, I'd been called a rich bitch after I said "Sorry" to a girl who'd asked me for change. And then a guy, who might have been one of the guys Amy was talking to right then, had been even ruder, asking if I would do him a certain sexual favor. Then he and the hostile girl had high-fived each other and laughed while I scurried away.

"Oh that's just a facade," Amy said when, a few minutes later, I tried to explain to her why I'd been hiding inside ShoeTique. I didn't tell her that I had also become quite interested in a pair of boots I'd seen in the window and was hoping to get back here with my mom to buy them later in the week. "It's really hard to live out on the street, Kels. They have to put on a tough front."

"Okay. But do they have to be so hostile?"

"You can't take it personally. Hostility is just a defense. They see someone like you walk by, with your shiny clean hair and your Banana Republic leather jacket —"

"Which I bought with my own babysitting money, by the way," I said, putting my hand on the jacket. "Thirty-three percent off. Plus another ten percent because of this." I held the bottom of the sleeve out for Amy to see the tiny rip at the edge that Mim had discovered and brought to the attention of the salesclerk when we were checking out.

Amy glanced at the edge of the sleeve and rolled her eyes.

"And since when did having clean hair become a crime?"

"Kelsey. You have a roof over your head, three meals a day provided for you, an apparently unlimited clothing allowance—" She was staring at the boot in my hand.

"Not unlimited—that would actually be a contradiction in terms: 'unlimited' and 'allowance.'"

"Okay, but you have a clothing allowance. Compared with these kids, you are definitely rich. You may not be a bitch—"

"I *may* not be a bitch?"

"I didn't mean that. Of course you're not a bitch. But you *are* rich, and you have a very privileged life. You could feed a whole village in Brazil for a year for what it costs to send you to Susan B. Anthony."

"Really?"

"I'm not sure. I'd have to look it up. The point is—and don't take this the wrong way, because I think you're really a great person—but you kind of live in a bubble. You've never had to even think about money or food or shelter in the way that these kids have to."

"And you have?" Saying this to Amy kind of scared me, because I wasn't sure if we were having a best-friends' tiff, or a friendship-ending fight. So far, we had never talked about the obvious fact that my family had a lot more money than hers.

Amy's dad had died when she was four, and her mom was a social worker at an agency in San Francisco. She and her older sister, Ruth, and their mom live in a small, rented two-bedroom house with only one bathroom. Their furniture is old, and the kitchen has never been updated. They don't even have a dishwasher. They're not messy, but the house has a very crowded feeling because there's just not enough room for all their stuff. Books are doubled up on the bookshelves in the living room, and videos and DVDs are stacked on top of the television. That one bathroom has enough tubes and bottles to fill a small drugstore. Their mom uses half the dining "room," which is really just an alcove, for her home office. The room that Amy and Ruth share is only a little bigger than the breakfast nook in my grandparents' house and maybe a little smaller than the dressing room of my parents' old master bedroom suite in Boston.

Amy shook her head. "No, you're right. I haven't either. I'm sorry. You can't help it if you were born rich."

I wanted to tell her that technically, I wasn't *born* rich. Dad was just starting his real estate business the year I was born. But by the time my brother, Josh, came along five years later, we were well on our way to what I guess most people would call rich.

I once asked my mom just how rich we were, and this was how she explained it: She said Dad could stop working that day and still support himself and us and her and a new wife and kids if that ever happened, sending everyone to private school and college and on good vacations. He could keep making his generous contributions to Harvard, where he hopes either Josh or I will go (which I'm not sure how I feel about, or how Harvard'll feel about, for that matter) and his other causes, like the single mother job-training program, anything to do with breast cancer research (because his mom died of that), and multiple sclerosis (because his best friend's wife has a really bad case of it).

"And he'd still have a good chunk to leave behind for you guys."

But the question of whether or not I was born rich was beside the point. There was no denying that my family had a lot of money. And while I wasn't sure that living in a small rented house with one bathroom for three females meant she was so much better able to understand life on the street than I was, I wasn't about to press that one either.

And so I let Amy's bubble comment hang there. I put the display boot down without asking the salesgirl to put a pair on hold for me. If they sold out before I was able to get back with my mom and her credit card, I figured it wasn't meant to be.

I followed Amy up Telegraph Avenue on her quest for the perfect used polyester pants.

4

Meet the Positive Parenting Partners

Applications for all the private high schools in the area were due January fifteenth. By early December, the eighth-graders at SBA had gone collectively insane. Though I still ate lunch with the sixth-graders, every once in a while I would catch bits and pieces of the eighth-graders' frantic talk.

"I'll die if I don't get into Scholastic," Melinda would say to Mallory, or vice versa.

"You are so going to Scholastic," Mallory would tell Melinda, or vice versa. "They wouldn't dare reject you."

Scholastic Academy was everyone's first choice.

According to Mrs. Myerson, competition was fiercer than ever.

"Being an SBA graduate will definitely up your

chances," she told a room full of us and our parents at a special meeting they had to coach us through the application process. "But you've got to put your best face forward."

My parents were sitting side by side in the front row with matching legal pads, each taking down every word about how to handle the interview, what to put in the personal statement, and whether to hire a private placement consultant.

I suppose I should have been pleased that my parents, who had spent the first year after their divorce not speaking, had improved their post-divorce relationship to such an extent that they were tackling the question of Kelsey's High School Options together.

The first year after they split up, they barely grunted at each other if they happened to cross paths at the parental changeover times. Usually, Mom just stayed in the house and Dad didn't get out of the car. If Mom called us at Dad's, he'd answer all cheerily, until he heard her voice. Then he'd just mumble "Yeah" and hand the phone to me or Josh. If they absolutely had to communicate about something, they did it by e-mail or with me as the messenger.

Then Mim stepped in.

She and Leonard, my grandfather, were visiting us not long after Dad moved out. One night, I overheard her and Mom talking in those hushed, tense tones adults use when they don't want you to hear them fighting. I crept to my listening spot out in the hall, where I knew, from years of eavesdropping on my parents' hushed, tense conversations, that I could hear without being seen.

Mim said it was ridiculous that Mom and Dad weren't speaking.

"We split up, Mom. We're exes. Of course there's going to be a little tension."

"You call not being able to stay in the same room long enough to hold a conversation about your children 'a little tension'? And if I want to say hello to my son-in-law—"

"*Ex*-son-in-law—"

"Oh, come on. I'm not going to start calling Larry my ex-son-in-law. We've been family for twelve years. I haven't seen him in months, and I'm not going to stand out in the cold to say hello because you guys can't figure out how to be in the same room."

"Mom. I know you mean well. But could you please back off?"

"You two should go see someone."

"What are you talking about?"

"I'm talking about someone who can help you communicate."

"I'm not going to therapy with my ex-husband. We did therapy. Therapy showed us it was time to call it quits."

"I'm not talking about couples therapy. This is something else. It's a new model that's specially aimed at exes with children. It's revolutionary. I know a great person. . . ."

"Mom, you always 'know a great person.' You know what? Not all problems are fixable."

I never heard the end of that conversation, because my mom's voice started getting louder, which meant she was headed my way, and I had to make a move, or get caught eavesdropping. So I strolled into the kitchen, opened the refrigerator, and in my best casual voice said, "What problems?"

"Were you listening?"

I shook my head at the milk carton in front of me. Which I know is technically still lying, but seems somehow less dishonest than looking my mother in the eye and saying "No" out loud. I grabbed the milk and shut the refrigerator door.

Mom looked at me while I got a glass out of the cabinet and said, "Nothing that concerns you."

× × ×

But a few weeks later, Josh and I were being dragged to Stan's office for a whole family meeting.

"He's helping us figure out how to have a relationship that isn't, you know, 'a relationship.' Your dad and I are always going to be related, through you guys, and we have to try to figure out a way to still be a family even though we aren't together-together."

Stan explained the "Positive Parenting Partners" approach to "post-divorce" life. There was a chart on his wall listing the Dos and Don'ts of Positive Parenting Partnerships. Stuff like, "Don't put the kids in the middle." And "Always be civil with each other. See if you can move on to cordial." "Be on time. Call if plans change."

It all seemed kinda lame and obvious to me. Not to mention expensive. The brochure in Stan's waiting room said he charged two hundred dollars a session with a minimum of ten sessions per family. I could have pretty much made the dos and don'ts list myself based on my experience.

But I have to admit, it helped. After a while, Mom and Dad started having little conversations when they found themselves on the phone. And then Dad started coming back into the house when he picked us up and dropped us off.

And now, ever since Mom started law school and was becoming a happier person, they seemed to be taking their post-marriage relationship to a new level.

Kind of brotherly-sisterly with a little bit of flirting now and then.

Which was beginning to squick me out. I mean, I was glad they were speaking. But the flirting I could do without.

Plus the Positive Parenting Partner thing was making it way harder to play them against each other. They were a unified force that would have made Stan proud.

× × ×

The three of us went to dinner after the meeting at SBA, and when I told them I wanted to skip the whole private school application process and go to East Bay High with Amy, they ganged up on me.

"We're not ganging up on you, honey," Mom said as the waiter cleared our plates. "We just don't want to see you closing off your options this early in the process. Right, Larry?"

"Right. Listen Kels, we just want you to be somewhere where you'll achieve your potential."

For my dad, "achieve your potential" means "get into Harvard."

Dad's a little nuts about schools.

It all goes back to his growing up semi-poor in Boston, and his mother not having any choice but to send him to the falling-down public schools in his neighborhood. For high school, he got accepted at Boston Latin, which is this famous, selective public school you have to apply for. (Matt Damon went there, too, by the way, but he hasn't yet shown up for any alumni events. I know, because Mom keeps asking Dad about that.) Dad said going to that school changed his whole life. It was his first stop on the road from rags to riches and he was determined that his children would have "every educational opportunity. . . ."

Mom told me how when it was time for me to start kindergarten, Dad insisted on checking out every school within a twenty-mile radius of our house.

"He drove himself—and me—crazy," she said. "He made a spreadsheet and ranked each school according to its teacher-student ratio, curriculum, and teaching philosophy. He grilled the teachers and admissions people before finally settling on Kendall."

I guess Dad's obsessiveness paid off, because Kendall had been a totally cool place for me. They worked us hard, but in a way that was fun. And even though it was private, it lacked the snot factor of SBA. Maybe that was because Kendall had a sliding-scale tuition. More than half the kids got financial aid. Whenever we went on field trips, everybody had to participate in raising money with car washes and raffle ticket sales, whether or not their parents could just write a check. Plus, we wore uniforms, and everybody took a city bus to get to school, so it wasn't so obvious who had money and who didn't. At Anthony, it was totally obvious who was on scholarship and who wasn't. If you couldn't tell by a girl's clothes, all you had to do was watch to see what vehicle she got into at the end of the day.

× × ×

After we ordered dessert, Dad opened his folder containing printouts from the Web sites of all the private schools, and a spreadsheet comparing their facilities and programs.

"How about Scholastic? They have an incredible curriculum. A great college placement record . . ." He handed me a brochure. Every picture contained beautiful kids from at least two different ethnic groups smiling at each other or the camera. Just like a Benetton ad.

"I want to go to East Bay High," I said, pulling

out the spreadsheet on which I'd done my own point-by-point comparison with information I got from the EBH Web site.

"Kelsey, honey, I don't think you realize how hard it is to get into the top colleges these days."

I pointed to the column that listed all the colleges East Bay High kids got into over the last four years, which included a respectable number heading for Harvard and Yale and those other places my dad worshipped.

And then, I couldn't resist. I played the guilt card: "Dad, honey? I don't think you realize how hard this transition has been on me. I would think you guys would be glad that I'm taking some initiative. Don't I have any say about my own life?"

They looked at each other.

"Seriously. Think about it. Everything that's happened over the last year has been because other people are doing what they want to do." I didn't look at Mom when I said this. But I could see her shaking her head out of the corner of my eye.

"Kelsey, it's always been your mother's dream to go back to law school. I thought you had gotten over that," Dad said.

"I have. Really." I looked right at Mom. "I'm very glad Mom is happy."

And she was. Even though she worked all the time, she was much more cheerful than she had been when she was mostly a housewife and mother whose main occupation was keeping track of all our activities and Dad's business trips and dinner meetings. Now she was just as busy as she'd always been, between studying at the law library and putting in hours at the immigration clinic where she interned, or meeting with her study group. She was busy, but she wasn't freaked out. By the end of her marriage to Dad, Mom's life was one big freak-out.

"I am really and truly happy that you are doing what you want to do. And now I'm telling you what I want to do: I want to make my own choices. I want to get out of this private-school bubble life I'm living in, which, though no one in this family believes me, is not all it's cracked up to be."

And then, mostly for shock effect, I told them how Serena Carter and Janna Coleman, another Melinda-Mallory wannabe, had gotten caught shoplifting at the Union Square Abercrombie & Fitch. Word from my sixth-grade sources was that Melinda and Mallory were behind it all. As in, the stuff Serena and Janna were caught with was for them. Serena's parents had managed to convince the store detective not to bring in the police, and now they were just hoping that word never got to Mrs. Myerson. Apparently, the year before, a girl had gotten caught shoplifting, and Mrs. Myerson had called all the private high schools the girl applied to and told them about it, and the only place that would take her was a therapeutic boarding school in Montana.

"Arlene doesn't know about it?"

"No. And don't tell her!"

"Someone should," Mom said. "That's a complete violation of the Honor Code."

"Hah, funny, Mom," I said, digging into my raspberry tart. "You don't think people really follow that, do you?"

"I hope *you* do," she said, giving me one of her looks.

One of the big selling points of the Susan B. Anthony Academy for Girls is its Honor Code. We have to sign a pledge on every test, report, and piece of homework we hand in, promising that we did it all ourselves. Plus we're supposed to be living our whole lives under the Honor Code, which means no lying, cheating, or stealing, even when we're not at school.

As far as schoolwork was concerned, I absolutely followed the code. And I would have whether or not there was a code. I do okay enough on my own and wouldn't want to hand in someone else's mistakes.

And I would never steal.

Now some people might say that's because I pretty much get everything I want. And while that isn't exactly true, it is definitely true that I've never known what it's like to really need something—like food or a winter jacket—and not be able to afford it. So maybe I shouldn't say "never" and just say that under my current socioeconomic circumstances, I would not steal.

The lying part? That was a little trickier. Because if you're going to get technical about it, of course I tell various sort-of and almost lies to my parents on occasion. But most of those are absolutely necessary, in-the-interest-of-family-harmony lies. Stuff like "No, I wasn't listening." How else is a person supposed to get vital information? Or "Yes, I promise I will finish all my homework before I go online." As long as the homework eventually gets done, what's the harm in a little IMing beforehand (or even during)? And if you're getting super technical, I suppose you could say that even the way I got all righteous and said, "Do you really have to ask?" when Mom asked if I followed the Honor Code could be seen as a kind of untruth.

"But you guys don't have to send me to a fancy

school to teach me to be honest. You taught me that." Hey, if the guilt wasn't doing it, I could always try sucking up.

They exchanged a look of pride, which seemed like a good moment to excuse myself.

"Why don't you talk this over while I go to the bathroom?"

× × ×

When I got back to the table, Mom was laughing, saying, "Larry, stop. You're going to make me pee."

"What's so funny?" I asked, slipping back into the booth next to Mom.

"Oh, nothing," Mom said, looking at Dad, who looked down at his coffee.

"Okay, so what's the verdict?"

They looked at each other and then at me and then at each other again.

"Well?" I asked, prepared for the worst, ready to repeat my best arguments.

Mom sighed. Dad shifted in his seat.

"Just tell me."

"We didn't talk about it," Mom said.

"You didn't . . ."

"You were back so soon," Dad said, which was

pretty lame, because I had deliberately taken my time, sitting down at the lighted mirror they had in the ladies' room, brushing my hair one hundred strokes, imagining them saying stuff like,

"She has had a rough year."

And:

"It's good she's showing some initiative."

Or:

"Maybe we should let her make her own decision here."

"What *were* you guys talking about?"

Dad looked at Mom and smiled. "Your mom was telling me about an interesting case she's studying. Listen, I have a proposal. We *will* let you make your own decision, but only after you've really explored your options. All we ask is that you take a tour of Scholastic. Sit in on some classes. So you know what you're passing up."

"Okay," I said. "As long as you guys are willing to come check EBH out with me."

"Deal," said Dad.

"Sure," said Mom, with a shrug. "Why not? I do think it's good that you're taking some initiative here, by the way, honey."

5

COMPARE . . .

A week later, Mom and Dad and I were traipsing through the shiny, sun-drenched, wood-and-glass buildings of Scholastic Academy behind perky senior Niki Wallace, who was applying to Harvard, Yale, Princeton, Cornell, Penn, Stanford of course, Georgetown, and all the University of California campuses.

"Wow," Dad said.

"Impressive list," said Mom, glancing my way.

"Yeah," Niki said, looking at me. "As I'm sure you know, the college counseling here is fantastic. It starts freshman year. You'll be assigned a college advisor as soon as you get here. Well, I guess I should say, *if* you get here. I know they're expecting a record number of applications this year."

I smiled my best imitation-hopeful smile and held up crossed fingers.

"Our first stop is the language lab," Niki said, nodding toward a window through which we could see twenty kids in glassed-in individualized cubicles, big fat headphones on their ears, speaking into the air.

"In addition to the usual—French and Spanish—Scholastic offers Italian, Japanese, Russian, German, and Gaelic."

"Gaelic?" asked Dad, widening his eyes.

"Yeah," said Niki. "It's something our founder wrote into the charter. His family came over here from Ireland during the potato famine. Even though he made all this money on the railroad, he wanted to make sure Scholastic always had a connection to his roots. I took it for a year, and it was really fun. Especially our trip to Ireland for spring break."

Dad elbowed me. "You hear that Kelsey-girl?" He was doing his brogue, which normally we only had to suffer through on Saint Patrick's Day. Dad's grandparents on his father's side were from Ireland. My name came from somewhere back in the Irish family tree. "Spring break in Ireland. Now doesn't that sound grand?"

"Come on, Larry," said Mom, rolling her eyes at me, but also laughing. "Don't embarrass your daughter."

That was all the encouragement Dad needed.

He put his arm around Mom and said, "Irish Spring. Manly, yes . . ."

Now Mom was out-and-out giggling.

This was getting ridiculous. Shouldn't there be some kind of law against former spouses flirting? At least in front of the offspring they've traumatized by splitting up in the first place? I wondered what Stan would have to say about this.

Adding to the creepiness of it all was the fact that Dad had just gotten serious with Carolyn, his future ex-fiancée. But instead of cooling off whatever was going on between my parents, Carolyn's presence in Dad's life seemed somehow to heat things up.

As we wound our way through the hills above Berkeley to Scholastic that morning, Dad had told Mom the ongoing saga of him and Carolyn and Carolyn's cats. He thought Carolyn should lock the cats out of her bedroom when he stayed over. Mom refused to take his side.

"Look Lar, the cats were there before you, and the cats will be there when you're gone. You're going to have to get used to it."

"But there's cat hair *everywhere*. On the pillows, sheets—"

That's when I lost it.

"Can you guys please stop? Please? This is torture. It was better when you hated each other."

"We never hated each other," protested Mom.

"We're just talking," said Dad.

"You're just talking about . . . sex," I said.

"Honey . . ." Mom said, stealing a look at Dad, who shrugged, like it was occurring to him that maybe they had crossed a line.

"You guys should go out on a date if you want to flirt. And Dad, you should tell Carolyn if you want to see other people."

"I'm not 'other people. . . .'"

"And your mother and I aren't 'seeing each other.' This is just our new, post-divorce family," Dad said.

"Whatever. Could you guys please just try to stay focused on the question of where I'm going to school next year? I'm only going on this tour because you two are making me. I already know I don't want to go to this school."

× × ×

Ever since my outburst in the car, my parents had been very careful. They'd avoided walking next to each other and were mostly talking to me or Niki.

Now, with Dad doing his brogue, they seemed to be lapsing back.

With one eye on Mom, he asked, "Would they be needin' any chaperones for that trip to Ireland, you suppose, lassie?"

Niki laughed politely but didn't answer Dad. She turned to me. "We're the only high school in the country that has a Gaelic program. It really helps us stand out in our college applications. Now, if you'll follow me, we'll go observe that class I told you about."

The class was AP English, in a fancy book-lined room they called the Founders' Library. Fifteen kids sat around a polished wooden table in heavy wooden armchairs, talking about shame vs. guilt in *The Scarlet Letter*. They all seemed to speak in perfect paragraphs, complete with topic sentences, supporting details, and what my sixth-grade English teacher called "clincher closers."

After that, it was on to the award-winning Scholastic Café.

"Wow. School lunch has come a long way since my day," Mom said, looking over the organic salad bar, where Scholastic girls—it looked like most of the school's female population was gathered there—

could choose from three kinds of lettuce, plus baby spinach and arugula. Also hard-boiled eggs, marinated mushrooms, artichoke hearts, green and black olives, sliced cheese, grated cheese, cold cuts, melon balls and fresh pineapple, low-fat, nonfat and regular cottage cheese, plus an assortment of dressings at varying fat levels.

I was hungry, and so I decided to join Dad and all the boys of Scholastic in the hot food line, where we could choose from roast chicken or, for the vegetarians, a cheese frittata, and for the vegans, a black bean and soy casserole. I piled my plate high with chicken, oven-roasted potatoes, and crusty French bread.

When we rejoined Mom and Niki, Niki was telling Mom how the café was the product of Scholastic students' activism.

"We walked out because the food was so bad. Nothing but fat and carbs." Niki's eyes widened at the pile of potatoes on my plate, but she recovered and continued her story. "The administration totally freaked. They were so afraid of bad publicity, they gave in to our demands right away. They put a student committee in charge of finding a new caterer. All the menus were developed with student input. It was very empowering. A real lesson in civil disobedience."

"Well, that's the old Berkeley spirit," said Dad, raising his fist and then, to my horror, starting to sing:

Power to the people.
Power to the people.
Power to the people.

When he got to the end of the fourth "Power to the people," he pointed to me and Mom and Niki, but only Mom answered with a giggly "Right on."

6

. . . And Contrast

"Officially it's called 'The Annex,' and the trailers are 'Temporary Portable Classrooms.'" Amy's sister, Ruth, led me and my parents down crumbling concrete steps at the back of the East Bay High campus. "But even the principal calls it 'The Trailer Park.' I mean, come on, who are we kidding?" Ruth spread her arms out over the rectangular pre-fabs below. Some were dull brown or gray, like the ones they use at my dad's construction sites. But a lot of them had been painted, some in wild-colored patterns, others with bright, densely packed murals.

"Mr. Rundle's is that double-wide back there." Ruth lifted her chin toward a bright purple-and-blue-striped structure at the farthest corner of what used to be a parking lot. If you looked closely, you could still see the faded white lines on the asphalt.

Ruth said we absolutely had to observe one of Mr. Rundle's classes. "He is just the most amazing teacher. Once you see him teach, you'll want Kelsey to go here. You might even want to go here yourselves."

Mom and Dad were looking a little shell-shocked as we walked by the portables.

"Looks like these things've been here awhile," Dad said, taking in the peeling paint and the rusty water marks around the edges of the metal windows.

"Yup," said Ruth with a shrug and a nod.

"When did you say they're starting the new building?" Mom asked, hopefully.

A few minutes before, she and Dad had been admiring the blueprints and model on display in a glass case in the lobby. Dad said he knew the architect.

"Hah," said Ruth. "They've been saying 'next year' every year that I've been here." Ruth was a junior. "It keeps getting postponed for lack of funds."

"Wow, look at this gorgeous artwork," Mom said, gazing at a mural on one of the portables.

It *was* gorgeous. Smiling teenage faces in every variation of skin color you could possibly imagine were painted standing and sitting in clusters and pairs, some looking sad and serious, others holding hands and laughing. One corner showed a couple sitting on a bench, forehead to forehead, staring into each other's eyes. In another corner there was a giant shiny silver boom box with musical notes pouring out of the speakers, floating above the heads of a group of smiling dancers. Off in another corner was a picture of a girl gazing into the eyes of a baby in her arms. The background was decorated with colorful flowers and butterflies and birds and—you guessed it—bees.

"That's the Student Health Center," Ruth said.

"Oh," said Mom, as she studied the mural. She smiled at the girls who were leaning on the railing in front of the health center, whispering. Then her eyes roamed over the mural, pausing over the picture of the girl and her baby. Mom snuck a quick look at Dad, who, oblivious to the mural, was busy counting the number of portables in the lot.

"This is such a waste of resources," he said, shaking his head. "People think it's less expensive to use these things, but they don't realize that the longer they postpone building, the more they're adding to their ultimate costs. Every year you delay, you're adding to the bottom line."

Just when it seemed we were going to move on to Mr. Rundle's room or trailer or whatever you call it without Dad's noticing the health center, Ruth said, "The EBH Student Health Center is famous. We've been on *20/20* and *Oprah*."

Dad shifted his attention from counting portables and shaking his head over the waste of money to listening to Ruth and looking at the mural.

"Really?"

"Yeah, we wrote the book on outreach and education on sexuality issues. Literally. Our guidebook is used by a bunch of schools."

"And you're involved with this?" Dad turned to Ruth.

"Yeah. I'm a Peer Health Educator. It's an amazing program we have here. It's all about kids helping kids. We offer pregnancy, STD, and HIV testing. We give out zillions of condoms—and lube. You'd be surprised how many kids know about condoms but not about lube. If you don't want the condom to break, you gotta use lube. And we basically just try to help kids take responsibility for their sexuality."

Ruth was so busy rattling off her various duties as a Peer Health Educator that she didn't notice how my dad was staring at the ground. He'd been doing okay until she said "lube." Then his face went totally pale.

Mom was studying the kids who were milling around in front of the health center—a group of mostly older girls, their skin color ranging, like the girls in the mural, across the spectrum. They were talking and laughing, totally oblivious to us or anyone walking by.

"Well I think it's great," she said. "If they'd had something like this when I was in high school, it could have saved a lot of heartache."

Ruth nodded. "Totally. It really makes a difference in our dropout rate. Pregnancies are way down. And the girls who do have babies? Most of them still graduate, because we have on-site day care." She pointed to another trailer way at the back of the lot decorated with animals and flowers. A few strollers were parked out front.

"Isn't that great, Larry?" Mom elbowed Dad.

He looked up, took a deep breath, and said, "Sure." He took a quick look at me and then looked away again. "Great. Now where's this amazing English teacher I've heard so much about?"

× × ×

Mr. Rundle's classroom couldn't have been more different from the Founders' Library at Scholastic. Although he had done what he could—taped up

New Yorker covers and postcards of famous authors—there was no disguising the fact that the room was a trailer and the wood "paneling" nothing but veneer.

"You're welcome to stay for the class," Mr. Rundle said, gesturing to the back of the trailer where there were a bunch of beanbag chairs and some big pillows. "Have you read Toni Morrison?"

I think he meant the question for me, but Mom answered.

"Oh, I love Morrison! My book group in Boston read all her novels one year. Which one are you doing?"

"*Beloved*," Mr. Rundle answered. "We tie it in with the U.S. history curriculum."

"Wow. What a great idea," Mom said.

"Make yourselves comfortable," Mr. Rundle said. "And feel free to join in the discussion."

"Thanks," Mom said. "Maybe I will."

I really hoped she wouldn't.

I didn't have to worry about Mom embarrassing me. There was no way my mom—even with her natural assertiveness and her new law-school training—could find an opening in the very heated discussion that followed. It was all about whether the slave woman in the book—who had killed her baby to keep it from being sent back to slavery—was guilty of murder.

Most of the class, which was about two-thirds white, said the woman was not guilty. They said the killing was done in a moment of madness, which made her not guilty by reason of insanity.

It seemed as if everyone was ready to agree to the "not guilty by reason of insanity" verdict until at the back of the room someone said, "Look, if my momma slit my throat, I'd come back and haunt her, too. She would never sleep again if I had anything to do with it. That lady is guilty as sin."

A girl in the front row said, "But, Jerry, she's trying to keep her baby from suffering."

Jerry scoffed. "From suffering? You tell me how taking a rusty old saw to a baby's throat gonna keep her from suffering."

"It keeps the baby from being a slave," the girl said. "The mother believes being dead is better than being a slave. She knows what it's like; she knows how horrible her kids' lives will be. She wants to save them from that."

"So killing her is saving her?"

"Yeah."

Jerry shook his head.

Things went around like that for a while, with

Jerry refusing to change his mind and failing to convince anyone else of his position. But Mr. Rundle somehow managed to keep things friendly, and every once in a while someone said something that made everyone laugh and broke the tension.

After the discussion, Mr. Rundle gave them a writing assignment: to explain how they would vote if they were on a jury. Was the character who killed her baby guilty of murder?

I wished I could go back the next day to hear how they all voted.

× × ×

Lunchtime at EBH is madness. They have an open-campus policy, which means you're allowed to go out to lunch. Downtown Berkeley has about a zillion restaurants and so, unless it's raining, pretty much everyone heads off for cheap burritos instead of the institutional fare offered in the cafeteria.

Ruth led us out onto the sidewalk, which was packed with EBH kids, all headed in the same direction, all talking, shouting, and laughing.

A girl walking in front of us squealed into a cell phone: "You did *not* say that to him." Then she turned around, searched the crowd, and started waving frantically, talking into her phone the whole time.

"Over here. Over here," she said, jumping into the air to get her friend's attention.

As we passed her, another girl with a phone joined her, saying, half into the phone and half to her friend, "Yeah-huh, I did."

Girl number one dropped her cell phone to her side. "Okay, spill."

I was dying to stay and hear, but I had to keep up with Ruth and my parents, who were discussing our lunch options.

"We can get Mexican, Chinese, Indian—" As Ruth presented our choices, there was a loud clatter up ahead, followed by a low roar that seemed to be getting closer. The crowd in front of us parted to reveal three guys rolling down the sidewalk on their skateboards. The one in the middle was eating sushi—with chopsticks—out of a plastic take-out tray while steering himself through the crowd and talking to the two guys on either side of him, one eating a burrito, the other some kind of meat on a stick.

"That sushi looks good," said Mom, as they rolled by.

The guy put his foot down on the sidewalk and stopped. He looked back at my mom, held a piece of sushi up with his chopsticks, and said, "Party Sushi, one block up. The Dragon Roll rocks." Then—it happened so fast I wasn't sure if I imagined it—his eyes shifted from my mom to me, and he smiled as he popped the sushi in his mouth. He pushed off the sidewalk, and rolled away.

"Who was that?" asked Mom.

"That," said Ruth, looking at his back, "is C.J. Logan."

"Big man on campus?" Dad asked.

"Oh, bigger than that," Ruth said. "He's a competitive skater—pretty well known. He was in the X Games."

"Wow," said Dad.

"And he goes to EBH?" I asked. My heart was pounding as if I'd just run a mile.

"Yeah," said Ruth. "He's a sophomore."

"Hmm," said Dad.

"So, Ruth," Mom said, "tell us about the extracurriculars. What are you involved with?"

"Other than giving condom lessons," said Dad.

"Larry, that's enough." It looked like Mom was beginning to remember how annoyed she used to get with Dad.

"Well, being a Peer Health Educator really does take up a lot of my time. Here we are." Ruth stopped and turned toward Party Sushi, a tiny place packed with EBH students. "But I'm also in a dance troupe and I do crew."

"Wow, that's a lot," said Mom, as the four of us squeezed in the door. "And you still have time for homework?"

"Yeah," said Ruth. "Barely. But I manage." Then she turned to me. "There really are an amazing number of clubs and activities. Our newspaper is considered one of the best in the state. We've got monthly poetry slams, fencing, a service club that works with Habitat for Humanity—just about anything you can think of."

"Ah, but tell me, lass, do they have Gaelic classes?"

This time, Mom just ignored Dad completely. Ruth looked at the floor and then back at Dad. "Ahhh no. No Gaelic. But we do have Latin. Most people take Spanish, which is the one language you don't have to leave California to use."

× × ×

By the end of the day, I knew more than ever that I wanted to go to East Bay High. It felt so much more alive to me than Scholastic did. Walking down its halls and up its stairs amid the slamming lockers and the "hey"s and "dude"s and "what up"s felt so much more like my idea of high school.

I didn't want to spend the next four years thinking about nothing but the next four years after that, which is how Scholastic felt to me—like no one ever talked about anything but where they were applying for college, or how something would look on their applications. And after the Susan B. Anthony Academy, I'd had it with small and intimate settings where you were either in or out, cool or uncool, with nothing in between.

East Bay High offered so many more possibilities of what I could become. Maybe I'd join the newspaper. Or help put on the film festival. Maybe I'd take up Indian dance or become a Peer Health Educator, though I figured I'd need a little more experience myself before trying to advise others on those matters.

7

I'll Take Skateboarding for Five Hundred, Alex

Little did I know the experience would come so soon.

Of all the lives I envisioned for myself as I filled out my registration form for East Bay High, Girlfriend of C.J. Logan, Mr. Sushi-on-a-Skateboard, Mr. Been-in-the-X-Games-and-on-the-Cover-of-*Thrasher,* wasn't one of them.

Sure, I knew I was pretty. I'm not going to lie and pretend I don't know I'm pretty.

I'm pretty.

There. I said it. And not because I'm conceited either. I just hate it when pretty girls pretend they don't know it.

It's bad form. If the gene pool has been nice to you, you should own up to it. Pretending you don't know is stupid.

The gene pool was nice to me. Even at almost forty, my mom is still pretty much a babe, and my dad is very good-looking, and when they got together, they made a pretty baby who grew up to be a pretty girl.

But I'm ordinary-pretty, not exotic-pretty. The people who say, "You should be a model" really don't know what they're talking about. You have to have freakishly big eyes or an extra-long neck or something that makes you stand out. And of course you have to be truly tall and totally skinny to be a model.

I'm just a tall*ish*—as in five eight—blonde, blue-eyed girl with a good metabolism. I can eat what I want—and I do—and still I'm on the thin side of normal. Now, if I were five inches taller and willing to starve, then maybe, with the help of a professional makeup person, I might get some work.

How do I know this?

Carolyn, my dad's aforementioned future ex-fiancée, brought me for a consultation with a friend of hers "in the industry." I think she thought she was going to score stepmother points by getting me a modeling job.

Well, that backfired. Big time. Her friend took one look at me and said that unless I grew five inches by the time I was sixteen, the only thing I could hope for would be the weekly Wal-Mart newspaper insert, and even then I'd be competing with hundreds of other ordinary-pretty girls.

Still, even though I knew I was pretty, I was surprised that someone like C.J.—a guy who could have his pick of any girl in school—would pick me.

× × ×

And he did pick me. Not vice versa as has been since claimed in his campaign of misinformation.

I was not hanging around the skatepark trying to get his attention.

And I never, ever stalked him.

The only reason I was even at the skatepark was because my mother forced me to go so I could keep an eye on my little brother. Josh had his own moving adjustment issues that year, and he was determined to get his skateboarding skills up to California speed by the end of the summer.

"Thanks, Mom, that's a great way to help me make friends—send a babysitter to trail along behind me." Josh was about as happy about the situation as I was.

"Oh, be quiet," Mom said. "And make sure his helmet stays on, Kelsey."

Josh rolled his eyes.

"I mean it, Joshua Samuel Wilcox. You think it's uncool having your big sister look out for you? Or wearing a helmet on a skateboard? Try wearing a diaper and having your big sister push you around in a wheelchair. 'Cause that's where a serious head injury will put you. And don't forget your knee pads and wrist guards."

Mom had just finished a course on personal injury law, and now she saw hazards lurking everywhere.

Josh and I worked out a deal: I would bring a blanket, a pile of books and magazines, my iPod, and my cell phone, and sit on the grassy field next to the skatepark minding my own business.

We would communicate on an as-needed basis.

× × ×

A skatepark is basically a big cement bowl, built to imitate an empty swimming pool. That's how the whole California skate scene started—in empty pools during a long drought in the seventies. (Thanks to C.J., I have a lot of random skateboard knowledge like that taking up brain space. Maybe it'll come in handy someday. Like, if I'm ever on *Teen Jeopardy*, I'll be able to say, "I'll take Skateboarding for five hundred, Alex.")

Berkeley's skatepark has something for skaters of all levels. The first bowl has a mellow shallow end, where five-, six- and seven-year-old beginners—covered head-to-toe in safety gear—wobble and fall and get chased around by their mothers, who tote first-aid kits and mini-coolers full of juice boxes and healthy snacks. The other end's deeper and steeper. That's where the kids Josh's age hang. From there they can study the more advanced moves of the serious Skater Dudes in the other bowl, next to which is a competition-grade vert ramp and a set of bleachers for demos and competitions.

Josh's problem was that he'd learned how to skate back East, where the scene was much less intense. His tricks were limited to what could be done on the handicap ramp of an office building near our old house (when the cops weren't chasing people away). Out here, kids Josh's age had been skating in real bowls since they were five, dreaming of entering the X Games at twelve or thirteen. Josh's best tricks weren't even considered tricks here—just stuff you did in between tricks.

He had a lot of catching up to do.

Even though I was mad about having to give up precious summer vacation time to watch Josh, I had to admire his determination. Watching him those first couple of afternoons, seeing how he kept getting up and trying again after each fall, even though the other kids hardly acknowledged his presence, made me feel proud of him and mad at them.

x x x

One day that week, I managed to convince Amy to come along. As soon as we got out of Mim's car, you could tell something was up at the park. There were a ton more people than usual. Not just skaters, either. The bleachers, which had been mostly empty the day before, were at least half full. And a lot of people in them were girls. Everyone in the park had their eyes on the vert ramp.

"What's going on?" I'd meant the question for Josh, but he had run ahead of us, and so the answer came from one of the Skater Moms, who had just come up behind us. She was walking fast, and as she passed us, she said, "C.J. Logan's here." She held a video camera in one hand and a mini-cooler in the other. Her little Skater Dude was running head of her.

"Oh." By then we'd reached the bleachers, in view of the vert ramp, where C.J. was flying up and across, soaring into the air and landing tricks with barely a wobble.

I turned to Amy. "Wanna check it out?"

"Not really."

"Why not?"

She held her hand out toward the pack of girls in the front row. Every time C.J. went up into the air, they'd squeeze each other's arms, letting go only when his wheels hit the wood again.

"Need I say more?"

"Oh come on, I just wanna see what they're all excited about." I grabbed Amy's hand and pulled her to the bleacher steps. She gave in and followed me to the top.

From up there, I understood the excitement. Every time C.J. flew over the ramp, I silently oohed and aahed along with the rest of the girls. When he finished his run, they clapped and whooped and yelled things like "I love you, C.J. I want to have your baby," which I thought was kind of a weird thing for a thirteen-year-old to say, even as a joke.

"Have you ever seen anything more pathetic?" Amy pointed to one of the Fan Club Girls running down the bleachers and over to the bench where C.J. was sitting, all so she could offer him a bottle of blue Gatorade.

"Really," I said, watching as C.J. turned around to take the bottle from the girl. He said something to her and turned back around to watch the guy who'd rolled down into the vert after him. C.J. took off his helmet and ran his fingers through his hair. "You have to admit he's hot, though."

"No I do not."

"Oh, come on. He's totally hot."

Amy raised an eyebrow. "Aha, I see. Maybe you should get a Fan Club application after all." She tilted her head toward the desperate girl standing behind C.J. She stood there smiling like an idiot for a few seconds and then skittered back to her seat to squeal with her friends.

"I'm just stating a fact."

"Uh-huh."

In some ways, C.J.'s your typical California boy, with blond hair made blonder by the sun (and in the winter by his mom's colorist, but you didn't hear that from me). He's tall and lanky and broad-shouldered, with arm muscles that are well-defined but not scary bulky like guys who live to lift.

Amy's taste in boys tended toward the less muscular. The wiry. The skinny. The bony. I shouldn't have been surprised that she couldn't see the C.J. Logan Factor.

But C.J. Logan is more than the sum of his parts. It's all about how he carries himself, how he seems to be floating through the air at all times, even when he's not flying above a vert ramp.

One word: smooth.

× × ×

Okay, so yeah, I admit: I was fully aware of C.J. before we officially met. But I was not hanging out trying to meet him, and I did not fake the event that finally brought us face-to-face a few days later.

I didn't even know he was at the park that day. If I had known, I never would have done what I did. I'm not into self-humiliation.

Here's what happened: I had read through all my magazines and hadn't been able to reach Amy on my cell, and so, out of boredom, I asked Josh to let me try a run. I'd done a little skating when I was younger. No tricks or anything. But I'd been able to make it down a straight ramp without falling. I wanted to see what skating in a bowl was like. Things were quiet that day; none of the older dudes were anywhere to be seen.

"Only if you wear this," he said, grinning, pointing to his helmet with one hand and wagging his finger at me with the other.

It's a good thing, too, because skating in a bowl is

way different from skating down a handicap ramp at an office building, and my first time up—well, "up" would be an exaggeration—I went splat. And clatter. And bang. And if I hadn't had that helmet on . . .

I didn't actually black out, but I finally knew what people were talking about when they said they saw stars after a fall. Not only that, but there was a ringing in my ears.

Josh was great. He didn't laugh or make fun of me. He ran to my side while the rest of the boys stood staring.

"Kels! Are you okay?"

"I think so," I said, inspecting my elbow, where I'd gotten a pretty good road burn. Spots of blood rose to the surface of both knees. One of the moms ran over from the shallow end, offering an ice pack.

"No thanks, I think I'm okay." I tried to smile through my wince.

Then the gawking ten-year-olds got quiet all of a sudden. I looked over to see a blond giant walk past their black-helmetted heads toward me. Well, next to them, and from where I was sprawled, he looked like a giant. Someone whispered, "C.J."

"Hey," said the giant, kneeling down next to me. "You okay?" The sun was shining right in my eyes, and I could hardly make out his face.

"I think so," I said. I reached under my chin to unclasp the helmet strap, which was too tight. I couldn't quite get ahold of the clasp.

"Do you know who the president of the United States is?"

"Huh?" The helmet strap felt tighter and tighter the more I fumbled with the clasp. Meanwhile, my elbow ached, my knees stung, my ears were ringing, and my butt hurt. And now C.J. Logan was asking me totally random questions. Maybe I had passed out. Maybe I was hallucinating.

"Hold up. I'll get it." He reached under my chin to unclasp the helmet, brushing his fingers against the soft, tickly underside of my chin. If this was a hallucination, it was a pretty detailed one. While pulling the helmet off, C.J. got between me and the sun and I got my first close-up glimpse of the green eyes, the blond hair, the green stone stud he always wore in his ear that just matched the green of his eyes. His right front tooth was chipped just a little off the corner.

Over the next year, I would come to know that chip intimately, and even now, after all that's happened, I still get a little tingly thinking about how its ragged edge felt against my tongue.

"Okay, so who is it?"

"Who is what?"

"The president."

"Um, why are you asking me that?"

"My dad's a neurologist," C.J. said. "That's the first thing you're supposed to ask someone who's banged their head: 'Who's the president of the United States?'"

"Why?"

"To see if there's been brain damage. Are you sure you know who the president is?"

"Yeah, duh. Everyone knows it's George . . . um, George . . . Washington."

I know, it was lame, but it was the only other president I could think of under pressure. I wondered why I felt the need to make a joke at that moment, and worried that maybe I'd inherited Dad's dumb-joke disorder.

I tried to push myself up off the ground, but plopped back down as soon as I felt the burning on my elbow.

"Hold up," said C.J. "Let me help." He squatted down behind me and was about to stick his hands in my armpits to pull me up. I hadn't shaved in a week, and I was more than a little sweaty—not to mention extremely ticklish—under there. I was wearing a tank, and just the thought of someone's hands in my damp, stubbly armpit made me lock my arms down. No sooner had I felt C.J.'s fingers touch the back of my shoulders than my elbows automatically jerked back. One landed right on his jaw.

Did I mention that this entire interaction was being witnessed by an openmouthed circle of ten-year-old boys? And that they kept stepping in, closer and closer, like Munchkins trying to get a better view of Dorothy?

The little Skater Dudes let out a collective "ooh" when my elbow hit C.J. in the jaw. C.J. himself made a sort of combination ugh-cough, keeled over, and started writhing around on the ground, rubbing his jaw and moaning.

"Oh my God, are you okay?" I stood up and leaned over him. His eyes were closed tight and his face was scrunched up. He held his jaw in his hand. "I am so sorry." I turned away from him and scanned the park for the lady with the ice pack. I spotted her off in the distance, packing her little skater into her SUV.

When I turned back, C.J.'s green eyes were open and looking right at me. "I'm fine. I was just playing. . . . What's your name?"

"Kelsey."

"Hey, Kelsey. I'm C.J." He reached up, offering me a handshake. "C.J. Logan."

"Hi, C.J.," I said in my most convincing really?-never-heard-of-you voice.

C.J. didn't let go of my hand when I loosened my grip. Instead he squeezed it tighter and sprang to his feet, making it look like I'd pulled him up.

"So . . . you taking up skating?"

"No. I'm just watching my brother, Josh." C.J. still hadn't let go of my hand. I held the helmet out to Josh with my other.

Josh stepped forward to take it. And it was only then, to shake hands with Josh, that C.J. finally let go.

"Hey, Josh. How's it goin'?"

Josh made no effort to hide his amazement. He just stood there, wide-eyed, as he shook the skating star's hand.

"What you working on, dude?"

"Oh, um, just . . ." Josh shrugged and looked down at his feet and kicked a pebble. "Still trying to land an ollie. But I keep slamming."

"Let me see it."

Josh looked up.

"Go ahead, take a couple tries. I'll see if I can figure out what you're doing wrong."

Poor Josh. I guess the pressure was too much. He didn't even come close to landing one. He rolled back looking even more embarrassed than before.

But then C.J. gave him this one little suggestion about timing and told him to try again. After slamming twice, Josh finally nailed his first ollie.

"Yes! You got it, little bro," C.J. yelled out into the bowl. "Now keep doing 'em until you don't even have to think about it." C.J. turned to me and said, "That's when you really know a trick—when you stop thinking about it. Your body just does it." He looked out at Josh, who had just fallen again. "That's all right. Remember—stay centered over the board and bend your knees before you land." Josh waved to C.J. and walked over to wait his next turn in line.

"So, will I see you and little bro here tomorrow?"

"I think. Maybe. Probably." Of course. Definitely. Positively.

"All right," he said, stepping backward. He pointed at my scraped-up arm and knee. "Get yourself some pads, and I'll have you flyin' in no time, too." Then he turned and jogged over to join his buddies by the vert.

It's a good thing his back was to me, 'cause I wouldn't have wanted him to see how long I stood there, watching him, wondering if what had just happened meant anything, or if it was the kind of thing that happened all the time in the life of C.J. Logan. It definitely wasn't the kind of thing that happened all the time in my life.

8

Dude, U Kick So Much Ass

Josh and I both went home that afternoon with visions of C.J. dancing in our heads. Over our dinner of take-out burritos, Josh tried to explain to Mim and Leonard just how big a deal C.J. Logan was. But the most he could get out of Mim was her generic grandmotherly vote of confidence: "I think that's terrific, Joshy."

Leonard was his usual grouchy self. "Is this guy one of the punks who chased the birds out of Hillside Park? Used to be one of the best birding spots in town. But now, between the noise of the wheels and the way those kids shout—nothing but crows and pigeons. Not to mention their language. If my mother ever heard me use such words? These guys don't care if there are little kids around, or mothers pushing strollers. It's 'f-this' and 'f-that' and 'f-you' and 'what the f?'"

Josh was frustrated. "You guys!" He was one notch down from shouting. "You just don't get it. C.J. Logan is huge. Huge." Josh got up from his chair and walked over to the kitchen computer. "Here, I'll Google him." Josh sat down, jiggled the mouse, and tapped something out on the keyboard. "Okay. Check this out. Seven hundred and seventy-one hits."

Josh might as well have been speaking Chinese to Leonard. It was only a few months before that we had managed to get him online at all. Now he's actually on the kitchen computer a lot, but he spends all his time at cyberbirders.com where crazy birding people brag about their life lists and send each other jpegs of their feathered friends. The number of Google hits someone's name brought up meant nothing to him.

I, however, was curious. And so after helping clear the table, I slipped upstairs to Google C.J. in the privacy of my own room.

Most of those seven hundred and seventy-one hits were just boring postings of contest results. C.J. had been competing since he was ten, so there were a lot of these. But I also found interviews with C.J. and articles about him on skating sites. Lots of pictures of him flying in the air above ramps all over California and the U.S., and also in Europe and Japan. There was a fan site kept by some anonymous girl who must have been a member of the Fan Club. She wrote about all of his competitions and posted reports of all C.J. sightings at the Berkeley skatepark.

Next I clicked on cjloganland.com, which I assumed was going to be another fan site. But it wasn't—it was C.J.'s blog.

I was surprised, because I'd always thought of blogging as a girl thing, filled with ramblings about crushes and fights with friends and mothers.

C.J.'s blog was all about skating. Skate contests. Skateparks. Skateboards. Other famous skaters and soon-to-be famous skaters. After I read all his recent entries, I combed through the archives, looking for something—anything—about his life outside of skating. The only non-skating-related entries were about sushi or C.J.'s very adorable dog Trippy, who I still love and miss very much.

The blog started the summer before, when C.J. traveled to Japan with a group of top U.S. skaters. He'd written something every day for the whole month of the tour, either about skating or the great sushi he was eating over there. After that, he wrote once or twice a week, mostly about upcoming contests or ones that had just passed. Some entries were basically essays on particular tricks, complete with background history and detailed how-tos. By the time I finished reading, I knew a little about the differences between California sushi and what C.J. called "the original real deal stuff" they made in Japan, and I understood how vert skating had been developed by surfers in Southern California who would skateboard in the afternoons when the waves weren't any good. Judging by the blog, there was no life outside of skating.

Which, now that I think about it, maybe should have been my first clue.

The comments on C.J.'s blog were something else entirely.

A bunch were from boys like Josh, who worshipped the wheels he rolled on:

Added by sosicksk8r

Monday, July 19, 9:24 PM

dude, u kick so much ass...keep it up

Added by s-man

Saturday, July 17, 10:57 PM

cj is the s—t i wish i was as good as him. he makes every thing look so easy

Added by kent675

Tuesday, June 08, 1:21PM

cj is the man...keep it up homie...call me up fool.

Added by jjkjj654321

Wednesday, April 21, 12:29 AM

and i will be skating i think cjs a pretty sick skater and he totally rips it up yea! yea hes tight thats all there is to it

Some were from rival skaters or fans of rival skaters:

Added by chomperfan

Wednesday, July 14, 1:40 PM

cj youve got some tricks that are pretty cool, and ill give it to you, you are pretty good, but all of you that say think he's the best in NorCal must not of seen chomper yet. i can quarentee you chomper is going places as well, big places

Added by chomper

Thursday, November 4, 12:20 AM

c u sat. prepare 2 looze dude.

But most of the comments were from girls:

Added by linsey and mary

Saturday, April 10, 4:17 PM

ur a hotttt skater.... u rip.... we want u....jd told u about us, so call us at ***-**** we love u

Added by rikki

Tuesday, March 02, 2:45 PM

cj ,hey u r a realy hot guy and a awsome skater . whens the next skate-comp.you will be at ? i wanna meet u

Added by qt4cj

Friday, February 27, 5:50 PM

cj...u r a grrrr8 sk8er and ur so totally hott! if u get a chance or if u even see this...im me at my aim (***grl13) lyl sk8 or die!!! <3 renee

Added by lollychick777

Friday, December 24, 12:46 PM

YEAH! i think your awsome....****** is my screen name IM me!!!!!! il sho u my tattoo.
-Brandie

I couldn't believe how many girls declared their "love" for C.J. online, begging him to IM them, leaving their contact info there for all to see. Some even put their phone numbers, which is like *the* number-one Internet safety violation. (Don't worry, I've changed the names and stuff to protect the stupid.)

Some girls left links to their own blogs and diaries, inviting (more like begging) C.J. to visit them online. I clicked on some of these. Most were the usual, predictable teenage blabbedy-blah. But some were scary.

As in basically pornographic scary. Girls posted pictures of themselves in bathing suits, thongs, and even less. Sometimes their faces would be in shadow, or only partially visible, but sometimes they were looking straight into the camera. Smiling! Plus, they wrote—in vivid detail—about the things they did with boys, the things they wanted to do with C.J.

I was grossed out, but also fascinated. Were these girls really doing all the things they bragged about? Maybe the diaries were more like creative writing exercises? The girls used screen names, but you could tell by some of the comments and guestbook entries that people from their schools knew who they were. Didn't they worry that their parents would find out?

But the biggest question in my mind was whether C.J. ever clicked these girls' links. (That sounds kind of obscene, doesn't it?) Had he dialed those phone numbers, taken lollychick777 up on her offer to show him her tattoo?

9

THE C.J. LOGAN FACTOR

Amy says I should let up on myself and stop focusing on my mistakes. Even she admits that it would have been hard to resist the C.J. Logan Factor.

"You never had a chance," she says, which is pretty amazing of her when you consider how bad a friend I was when I was with C.J. "Especially after he used that caveman hair-grab move. You just weren't yourself after that."

Okay. Technically, C.J. did grab me by the hair one afternoon and yes, I did pretty much lose it after that. But it wasn't a caveman hair-grab. It was much more subtle, and I should never have told Amy about it.

It happened a couple of weeks after Josh and I first met C.J. at the park. While I kinda sorta thought maybe C.J. liked me, I still wasn't sure. For all I knew, he gave skating lessons to ten-year-old boys and their older sisters all the time. Just because he talked to me and didn't talk to the Fan Club Girls didn't necessarily mean anything. And with all those girls throwing themselves at him on his blog, he wasn't exactly hurting for female companionship.

This particular afternoon, C.J. and I were sitting on a bench watching Josh take his last run of the day. (With C.J.'s help, Josh had become quite the little Skater Dude, and having C.J. Logan as his private tutor had helped Josh's image in the eyes of his peers.) Mom was picking us up that afternoon and had made a big deal about our being on time. I glanced at my watch and realized Josh and I had only two minutes to get to the other end of the park, so I jumped up to get Josh's attention. The next thing I knew, C.J. was standing next to me. He reached out, swept his hand across my neck, and gathered my hair into a bunch. Then he used my hair to pull me back down to sitting so close I was practically in his lap.

"Whoa, whoa. Hold up. What are you doing later?"

Despite the fact that C.J.'s hand was resting on the back of my neck and every inch of my body was covered in goose bumps, I managed to squeak out, "Um . . . just hanging with Amy."

"Yeah? Where?" And then he spread his fingers out and ran them through my hair, and I had to kind of gasp for air.

"Nowhere. I mean, at home."

"Maybe you guys could meet up with me and Flip at The No. They got some good bands playing tonight." He twisted my hair into a little knot and then let go, so that it fell around my shoulders.

"Maybe," I managed to say, wondering:

a.) How I was going to explain my sudden interest in The No to Amy, who had been trying to get me to go there with her forever;

b.) How we were going to pitch it to my mom, who was still very hazard-wary; and

c.) Whether my legs would ever work again. They felt, as the saying goes, like jelly.

× × ×

The No, a.k.a., ClubNoTrouble, is this sort of famous, kind of punky, all-ages club in Berkeley run by a bunch of Straight-Edge kids. Amy had been going there with Ruth since she was twelve, and she'd been trying—unsuccessfully—to get me there for months.

But she took it in stride.

"Okay, I'm not exactly thrilled that it's taking a

boy to get you to check out the place I've been begging you to go to for, like, ever, but I am glad that you're finally going." Amy plopped herself and the worn brown grocery bag she was carrying down on my bed. The plan was for Ruth to drop me and Amy off and we would meet C.J. and his friends there. "Um, you realize you cannot go dressed like that."

"Like that" referred to my basic uniform of jeans—which I admit were a bit tight and kind of low, but not any tighter or lower than what most girls wear these days—and my standard scoop-neck, cap-sleeve T-shirt, which I own in a zillion colors. I'd chosen lime green that night, to go with the chunky lime-green-and-orange flip-flops I'd bought that afternoon.

"What?" I glanced in the mirror. "I know this isn't exactly the height of punk fashion, but I figured it was generic enough."

"Ummmm, no," said Amy, digging into her grocery bag. One by one, she took out the items of my alterna-outfit: big black canvas work pants, a black long-sleeved thermal shirt, plus one of her ripped-up Salvation Army Special T-shirts to wear over that. I hadn't seen this one before: black with a white horse and white letters that said, HAPPY STABLES, DURANGO,

COLORADO. It looked like it would be about two sizes too big for me. For footwear, she'd thrown in a pair of black, paint-splattered slip-on Keds.

I picked one up and stuck my finger through the hole at the big toe.

"Aren't those great? My grandmother was going to throw them away."

"Oh." *How great that you caught her just in time.* "Um, am I allowed to wear socks?" Of all the used items I planned on never wearing, shoes topped the list. I'd actually sat out of several bowling parties when I was little because Mom refused to buy me my own pair of bowling shoes and I refused to wear the Lysol-drenched rentals.

Amy shrugged. "Suit yourself."

I put everything on and let Amy make adjustments. She pushed up the sleeves of the thermal shirt, pulled on one of the tinier holes in the T-shirt to make it bigger, and then stepped back to take a look at her efforts.

"We've got to do something about the hair. You still look like a cheerleader."

My hair's very straight, and it pretty much stays that way all day long, no matter what I do to it.

"Wait, I have just the thing." I headed out my

door, down to my mom's room. The last time we'd gotten haircuts, our stylist had sold us a bottle of some supposedly magic stuff that allowed you to shape your hair any way you wanted. I ran down to Mom's room, found the bottle on her dressing table—which was something of a challenge, considering the number of bottles and jars lined up in neat rows—sprayed it all over, and gave it a quick, ten-finger tousle.

Amy was not impressed. "Okay, now you look like a cheerleader who just woke up from her power beauty nap. You need a hat. What do you have?"

I showed her the assortment of knit caps I kept in a basket by my bed. One by one she rejected them all.

"Too new. Next?"

I tried another.

She shook her head. "Too Gap."

"Actually," I said, "it's Old Navy, and I got it on sale for three ninety-nine."

The next one was "Too cute. Way too cute. What about Josh?"

"I don't think—" But she was already out the door, heading toward Josh's room.

Josh's favorite hat was a maroon-and-white trucker cap with some skating logo on the front. My mother was always begging him to let her wash it, but he refused, saying it was bad luck. He'd never let me wear it. Which was fine with me.

While Amy was gone, I studied myself in my full-length mirror. Not as bad as I had thought. At least you could still tell I was a girl. And the clothes were perfectly clean, even if they were previously owned. I stared at the Happy Stables shirt, wondering who else had worn it and under what circumstances. A happy horsey girl maybe, whose grandmother picked up the shirt while traveling around in an RV on her honeymoon with her second husband, Ralph. Or maybe the shirt belonged to some guy who worked at the stables, fighting off flies while he shoveled up after some happy horsey girl's horse.

I wasn't about to convert to Amy's used-only clothes policy, but for the first time, I saw the appeal. I could see how you could get into it, assembling a whole wardrobe of one-of-a-kind items, each with its own history. Now that I thought about it, half the stuff at Abercrombie was fake-used. T-shirts with old-fashioned pictures and ads, and jeans made to look like they'd been worn for years. Weird.

Amy burst back into my room. "Here we go," she said, throwing something green at me. A bright green—as in Saint Patrick's Day green—knit cap I'd never seen before.

"Do I have to?" I asked, holding it in front of me. Lately, Josh had been letting his hair get as greasy as possible, going for some kind of punk-grunge-skater effect. Who knew what lurked on those synthetic green fibers? Plus, as much as I was getting into this new look Amy was creating for me, I really didn't want to cover up my hair.

"Of course you don't *have* to. It's up to you."

I looked in the mirror. Suzy's Miracle Volumizing Styling Spray had left my hair a stiff, crackly mess. I pulled the hat down over my forehead.

Three short honks told us Ruth was out front.

"Come on," Amy said. "We've got to move. I had to blackmail her into driving us, and she's not happy."

"Okay," I said as I reached into my closet and grabbed my leather jacket.

Amy stopped and looked at me.

"Um. What do you think you're doing?"

"Have you seen that fog out there?"

"Yeah."

"So, I don't want to freeze waiting in line."

"Uh-huh. Well you can't wear that."

"Oh come on, I did everything you said, Aim. Can't I just—"

"No."

"But . . ."

"No, I'm serious. I'm not talking about style, Kels. It's one of the Nos: No Dead Animal Anything."

"You're telling me that no one in that club tonight will be wearing leather shoes?"

"Well, they're not supposed to, but no one messes with you about your shoes. They will mess with you about that jacket, though. Big time. If you wear that jacket, we won't get in."

"But I thought the whole thing about this club was that they didn't exclude anybody?"

"Yeah, well, nobody within reason."

I threw the jacket on the bed and followed Amy downstairs.

My mother intercepted us before we could get out the door. One hand on her hip, the other wagging a finger, she said, "Remember . . . I want you two back inside this house—not driving up, not walking toward the front door, not even turning the front doorknob, but *inside the house*—by eleven. Do you understand me?"

Amy still wasn't used to my mom's dramatic ways. She nodded, all wide-eyed.

"Yeah, Mom, don't worry. We will be."

"I mean it, Kelsey. Or else you will be doing nothing but renting movies on Friday and Saturday nights for the rest of your teen years."

"Mom, don't you have some studying to do?"

Amy looked shocked, until my mom leaned over and kissed me. "Hah hah, very funny. Have fun. Be good! Have *good* fun."

10

"Let's Go Outside and Talk," and Other Lines I've Fallen For

C.J. had said not to worry.

"I'll find you," was how he put it, with a final stroke to my hair.

After waiting in line for twenty minutes, Amy and I finally paid our cover and walked in. Everyone, it seemed, was wearing all or mostly black, and from the looks of it, mostly used clothes. C.J. would have to be wearing Day-Glo orange for me to find him.

I was a little worried.

Amy wasn't. She was excited. ZooBabes, one of her favorite bands, was about to start their set. I tried to focus as she explained how the four girls had met when they were all working in the snack bar at the San Francisco Zoo. In between spinning cotton candy and popping popcorn, they'd started writing their songs, which all had something to do with animals. I half listened, while scanning the room for C.J.

Before Amy finished the ZooBabes history lesson, the band ran onstage. Amy grabbed my hand and pulled me behind her as she fought her way to the front of the dance floor. Now I had the choice of standing there like an idiot or joining the mass of humanity writhing around me.

Joining the writhing mass was a lot easier than I thought it would be. The ZooBabes played an incredibly fast, almost frenzied style that you couldn't help but move to.

Once I started dancing, I didn't want to stop. I decided to trust that C.J. would find me. So I danced, through "Giraffe-o-topia," "Lion's Den," and "Z-Z-Z Brr-A-A-A!"

Normally, I hate to sweat—except at kickboxing class. But here, it actually felt good. By the end of the first set, the thermal shirt Amy had dressed me in was totally soaked through and the Happy Stables T-shirt was well on its way. And I'm pretty sure that if I'd wrung out the leprechaun hat, it would've made an actual puddle on The No's concrete floor. I was a little afraid that with so much used clothing around me, the place would start to smell. But when the set ended, they opened the huge garage door at the back of the club and a wave of cool, foggy night air washed over us.

ZooBabes' lead singer announced they'd be back after a short break, and I followed Amy toward the back of the room for water. There was a row of industrial sinks where the regulars were filling their Nalgene bottles. Or you could buy a 100 percent recycled paper cup for a quarter and write your name on it with one of the markers tied to the wall with string. Handwritten signs along the wall urged us to throw our cups away in a recycling bin when we were finished. The No is very environmental and very organized.

While Amy went off to buy us cups, I finally spotted C.J. He and Flip were across the room, surrounded by girls. I recognized a couple of Fan Club members. Flip was doing most of the talking, while C.J. scanned the crowd. At one point, he seemed to be looking right at me, and so I waved. But C.J. just lifted his chin and continued to search the room. I couldn't find Amy, and I didn't want to freak her out by disappearing, so I waited and kept my eye on C.J.

I watched as a few different girls came up to him. He'd nod or lift his chin, and then look back out into the crowd. The girl would stand there for a minute or so and try saying something else. He'd turn back, give her a one- or two-word answer, and then look into the crowd again. Eventually, the girl would give up and move on, only to be replaced by another, and the routine would start again. C.J.'s eyes passed in my general direction two more times and I waved to no avail. He must have thought I was just another Fan Club member, because after that chin lift, he seemed to be purposely avoiding eye contact with the frantic waver across the room.

It was frustrating to not be able to get his attention. But in a weird way, it also felt exciting to watch as other girls standing right in front of him failed to get his attention, too. Knowing he was looking for me—even as he was looking right through me—gave me a thrill.

Yeah, I know. That's messed up. I can totally see it now. But at the time? What can I say? I just wasn't capable of such insight.

Finally, Amy came back with our water, and I was free to walk across the room to say hi to C.J.

Amy said she'd wait for me. She'd met some girls who'd followed ZooBabes on their tour, and they were telling her about the shows in Wisconsin and South Dakota.

When I got there, C.J. was ignoring yet another hopeful contender. After she left, he ignored me, too, not even looking at me when he said, "Hey," back to my "hey."

So I said, "Do you know who the president of the United States is?"

That got his attention. He looked at me. And then leaned in, as if he couldn't quite see.

"Kelsey?"

"Yeah," I said. I reached up to my head, thinking I'd rip the hat off and reveal my true self. But then I remembered the condition my hair had been in when I'd last seen it. An hour of sweating inside the leprechaun hat couldn't have improved matters, so I just sort of adjusted it instead.

C.J. reached out and touched the bottom of the T-shirt. "What's this? Kelsey goes punk?"

"Yeah." I shrugged. "I owe it all to Amy," I said, pointing across the room to where Amy stood laughing and talking with the ZooBabes fans. "What do you think?" I took a twirl.

He brought a hand to his chin and leaned back to study me. "I don't know. . . . You look a lot different. Turn around again."

While I spun around, C.J. reached out for the T-shirt, and used it to pull me right up next to him.

He slipped a hand into my back pocket, put his mouth up next to my ear and said, "Where'd that nice ass of yours go?" He spread his fingers out inside the pocket and pressed in. Hard. "Ah . . . there it is."

Up to this point in my life, I'd never had a guy's hand in my pocket, or a guy's lips on my ear, let alone both of these new sensations at the same time. Plus, while I'd never had reason to think my butt *wasn't* nice, no one had said that it was. Not like that, at least.

Repeating his words in the cold light of knowing what I know now, I can see how someone might think that maybe this wasn't the first time C.J. had executed this particular trick, and that mine wasn't the first ear he'd said such things into.

But you know what? I liked it. And at the time, I didn't care how many ears he might have whispered in before mine.

It was too dark for anyone to notice, but I was way beyond blushing. This was something else altogether. I could feel blood rushing to my face, my chest, and parts of my body I didn't usually pay attention to. C.J. pulled me in so that my nose and lips were up against the soft skin of his neck, which smelled like a mix of soap and sweat. Which may sound gross, but which—trust me—wasn't. I had to fight the urge to open my mouth and bite. Blood pounded in my ears, muffling the sound of the crowd yelling and clapping.

ZooBabes were back from their break. C.J.'s hand was still in my pocket and I couldn't move.

As if from far away, I heard a familiar melody played on the keyboard. I knew every note, but I couldn't think of the words. Around me I heard people walk toward the dance floor.

Knowing Amy must be looking for me, I forced myself to pull away from C.J.'s neck. I turned around and sure enough, she was looking right at me. Glaring is more like it. She held her hands out to say, "Are you coming?"

I shook my head slowly, scrunching my mouth up and squinting, hoping to convey the message, "I'm sorry. Don't hate me."

She scowled, rolled her eyes, and turned away, joining the circle of ZooBabes fans surrounding the keyboard player.

I closed my eyes and leaned back into C.J. He leaned his face into my neck. His left hand still hadn't come out of my left pocket. Now he took his right arm, crossed it over my right shoulder, and slid his hand across my belly. For a second, I worried that he'd be grossed out by the sweat. But it didn't seem to bother him.

And it wasn't bothering me anymore, either. Nothing was. I was standing in the middle of a crowded club pretty much, as the saying goes, wrapped in C.J. Logan's arms.

I knew that song. What was it? The keyboard player went through the melody a few more times and then stopped.

The room was silent. I opened my eyes. The whole place was dark, except for a spotlight on the lead singer. She had changed from the black T-shirt and jeans she wore in the first set into a beautiful vintage-y red dress. She started to sing, in a slow, breathy voice: "*If we could talk to the animals . . . just imagine it.*"

The girl could sing. When she got to the part about chatting in chimpanzee, the *eeee* went on forever, and between the sound of her voice and the weight of C.J.'s hand in my pocket, I felt like I was in a dream. Suddenly all the stage lights went back on, and the guitar, keyboard, and drums came in, picking the pace up to where it had been in the first set. The dance floor exploded. I could see Amy, a huge smile on her face, hopping around with the other girls in front of the stage, screaming out the words to *Doctor Dolittle*'s theme song.

I took a step toward the dance floor, expecting C.J. to follow, but he pulled me back by my pocket.

I turned to him. "Don't you want to dance?"

He shrugged and pulled me in closer. "Not right now. Let's go outside and talk."

Part of me wanted to pull his hand out of my pocket and run, to join Amy and her new friends and dance and sing "Talk to the Animals" until I soaked my clothes all over again.

But this other part of me wanted to breathe in C.J.'s sweet soapy smell and hear him whisper, "Nice ass," again and again.

I went outside.

11

Outcast No More

That night wouldn't be the last time I ditched Amy for C.J.

Lucky for me, she's a forgiving person. And lucky for me, she got totally into Drama Club. While I spent my freshman year starring in the role of C.J. Logan's Girlfriend, she was busy perfecting the parts she got in that year's productions—*The Pajama Game* in the fall and *The Crucible* in the Spring. And getting to know a Retro Punk Vegetarian-going-on-Vegan Drama Nerd (and ZooBabes fan) named Gabe, a situation that would, alas, come to its own bad end.

Amy was totally pissed at me about that night at The No. But not because I passed up dancing with her for making out with C.J. in his truck.

"I knew you weren't going to dance with *me* all night once Mr. Skateboard God showed up. But I thought that maybe you would have had enough sense—and consideration, by the way—to come back in time for our ride. Especially after what your mom said."

She and Ruth had to search the streets around the club to find C.J.'s truck, and once they did, we had all of ten minutes to make it back by my mom's deadline, and Ruth, who had just finished a traffic safety training course for her Peer Health program, refused to speed, so she and Amy fought all the way home while I stared out the window in an altered state of consciousness, running my fingers over my swollen lips, reliving my first moments alone with C.J.

× × ×

As for sense and consideration, I didn't demonstrate much of either freshman year. All those excellent reasons I had for wanting to go to East Bay High went right out the window as soon as I started hanging out with C.J.

I did okay in my classes. SBA had put me a little bit ahead in math and science, so I didn't have to work that hard in geometry or biology to get my Bs and B-pluses. And lucky for me, I got Mr. Rundle for

English. That was the one class I got an A in, and Mr. Rundle gets all the credit. He makes it impossible for you not to get excited about discussing the books, and he also makes it impossible for you to fake your way through those discussions.

But I didn't get involved in any of the extracurriculars I'd been so psyched about and used to convince my parents to let me go to EBH. All my free time went to C.J. I'd hang out at the park on weekday afternoons, sometimes skating with him, but mostly sitting by myself or with other guys' girlfriends, watching and waiting. Most weekends were taken up with going to C.J.'s competitions.

Over Christmas break, Mom and Dad sat me down and tag-teamed me about it.

"C.J. is a great guy," said Dad.

"And his family is terrific," Mom added. C.J.'s parents had invited my entire family to their annual holiday cocktail party, and our moms had bonded over a low-carb eggnog recipe. "But you told us you wanted to go to EBH because of all the activities, and you haven't joined a single one."

"I'm not *not* paying all that tuition for you to waste your time." Dad's lame joke sent Mom into hysterics. This was around the time Dad and Carolyn got engaged, and Mom and Dad's post-divorce relationship seemed tighter—and weirder—than ever.

"We've discussed it." Mom looked at Dad. "Right, Larry?"

Dad nodded.

"Get involved in something. Anything. Or . . ."

"We'll have to revisit the school-choice policy."

And so I joined the very undemanding yearbook staff. I sold candy bars at lunch sometimes to help raise money, and took the pictures and wrote the profiles of the cafeteria ladies. That part turned out to be more fun than I'd expected. I interviewed each lady and put little quotes from their life philosophies along with the recipes for their favorite menu items under their pictures. The cafeteria ladies liked me for taking an interest in them, and on those rare occasions when I bought lunch at school, they'd slip me extra fries or double whipped cream on my strawberry shortcake.

But other than that, I didn't exactly immerse myself in the throbbing, multicultural world of East Bay High.

I didn't try to meet new people. I barely even tried to hold on to the one friend I already had.

I hate to admit this, because I'd like to be able to tell you that my year of loneliness at the Susan B.

Anthony Academy for (Mean) Girls helped me to see how superficial and stupid labels were and how destructive cliques could be.

But you know what?

I loved being C.J. Logan's Girlfriend.

I loved the status—walking across the courtyard to join him and his friends on the first day of school and seeing the sophomore and junior and even senior girls looking my way while pretending not to notice or care. I only wished Melinda and Mallory could have seen how C.J.'s otherwise closed circle opened up when I approached, and how C.J. put his arm around me and pulled me to his side.

Of course C.J. never said much to me when he pulled me to his side like that. Usually he just went right on talking with his buddies. They'd review the latest skating news or trash rival skaters. Sometimes they'd forget I was there, and Flip or S-Man would talk about the girls they'd hooked up with at some party, and then I'd elbow C.J., who'd make them shut up. I didn't think much of it at the time. I figured the girls in question were like the ones who were always throwing themselves at C.J. at the skatepark and online, so what could they expect?

As long as I felt the weight of C.J.'s arm across my waist or his hand in my back pocket, I was happy, and I didn't question things. I was C.J. Logan's Girlfriend, plucked from obscurity to be the chosen one of a guy who could have chosen anyone. A mere freshman with the most popular junior guy for a boyfriend.

Kelsey the Eighth-Grade Outcast was a thing of the past.

I loved going to skating contests—watching and cheering while C.J. competed, holding his hand while he waited for his scores. I was even on TV for a few seconds a couple of times! Word got around pretty quickly that C.J. had a girlfriend, and so the Fan Club Girls stopped trying to win him over with bottles of Gatorade, and girls stopped trying to lure him into IM relationships and inviting him to visit their NC-17 diaries.

I didn't mind that there was so much waiting and watching involved in being the girlfriend of a Skater Dude. I didn't mind that sometimes C.J. had no time for me because he was training for a big contest. Because I knew that after the contest was over, the two of us would get into C.J.'s pickup and drive to our spot on Grizzly Peak, this road high in the Berkeley hills, with amazing views of San Francisco Bay, the Golden Gate Bridge, and San Francisco. When we were at our spot, we were in our own world.

So for most of a whole year, things were fine. Better than fine.

And then, slowly, the thrill of being C.J. Logan's Girlfriend started to wear off.

C.J. and I would have these hot Saturday nights at our spot, and over the course of almost a year, they got more and more advanced. Then we wouldn't see each other—except at school, with tons of people around—for three, four, or five days. We'd talk on the phone and IM and stuff, but we were never really together, just the two of us, except in the pickup. Amy's rehearsal schedule was at its most intense, and when she wasn't practicing her about-to-be-hanged witch's screams, she was hanging with Gabe.

There I was, on or near the top of the social food chain, and I felt lonely. Not that I was ready to admit this to anyone but myself, in the quiet of my own room, late at night, just before falling asleep. When day came again, I'd go through all the motions.

Then three things happened, that, together, made it impossible for me to continue to pretend everything was cool.

The first was on a night C.J. and I went to a party after a competition in Sacramento. It was in this amazing house in a gated community with an indoor swimming pool and a live band. But even in that fancy setting, the party consisted of the usual: Skater Dudes getting drunk and yelling at one another. C.J. never drank when he was driving, but that didn't keep him from yelling along with the others. I spent most of my time sitting by the side of the pool, dangling my feet in the water with the other Skater Dude Girlfriends, talking about our boyfriends.

In the middle of some girl's story about how her boyfriend got a contract for a Mountain Dew commercial, Amy called me from backstage after the final performance of *The Crucible*. In tears. (I'd gone to two of Amy's three performances, but had opted out of the final one so I could go to this party with C.J.)

"He's going to break up with me, Kels. I can tell."

"Gabe? No way."

"There's someone else. I can tell. He's been making all these calls on his cell, and hanging up when I come near."

"I'm sure there's some other explanation."

"Plus he hasn't kissed me in a week."

"I saw you guys kissing yesterday."

"That was *me* kissing him. Big difference. I think it's this girl Giselle. She's always looking at him when she thinks I'm not looking."

I wasn't worried—Gabe hadn't struck me as the kind of guy who would,

a.) Be able to attract the attention of two girls at once, or even if he did;

b.) Actually dump a girl like Amy who he was so lucky to have.

While I was talking to Amy, C.J. sat down next to me, put his feet in the water and started playing footsie with me. "Where you been? I've been looking for you."

I put my hand over the phone. "Just a sec—I'm talking to Amy."

He rolled his eyes and turned his back to me.

"Aim. I really doubt Gabe is going to dump you. Where is he right now?"

"Um, he went to get his car, and he's going to pick me up and we're supposed to go to the cast party."

"See? If he was going to break up with you, I hardly think he'd be making plans to go to a party with you."

Amy groaned.

"Call me back if you need to, okay? If not, I'll call you when I get home, 'kay?"

"Okay," she sniffled.

Just after Amy and I hung up, my mom called to

make sure I was going to be home when I said I would. Which I always was and which she continued to badger me about anyway. And then my dad called, because he was coming into town in the middle of the week and wanted to have dinner.

And so when C.J. buried his head in my neck and whispered in my ear, "Why don't you turn that thing off for a while?" I did.

The thing is, I forgot to turn the phone back on, and when Amy called an hour later, she got my voice mail. And I was so tired by the time C.J. dropped me off that I went right to bed without checking my messages. In my own defense, I should emphasize that I really thought Amy was imagining things. It wasn't until the next morning that I heard Amy's weepy message on my voice mail, choking out the news that she had caught Gabe making out with Giselle at the party, and that Gabe had then dumped *her* before she could beat him to it.

I called her as soon as I heard the message.

"Where were you?"

"There's no reception on the way home from Sacramento."

"Okay . . . and when you got back to town?"

"I, um, I—"

"I can't believe you didn't even check in with me. Do you have any idea how I felt last night? I couldn't get hold of my mom, and so I walked home."

"Really?" That was dangerous. Thank God nothing happened to her. If I had turned my phone back on or called Amy back to see how she was doing, I might have been able to get Mim or Mom to go pick her up. I thought back. What had I been doing while Amy was trying to call? Making out with C.J. on the balcony of some guy's house, some guy whose name I didn't even know. Or maybe by then C.J. had abandoned me again to go talk to the guys and I got stuck listening to Julie, Flip's girlfriend, go on and on about what hard-asses she thought the judges had been that day and how Flip should have placed second instead of fifth.

"Amy, I never in a million years thought Gabe could possibly dump you," I said, leaving off the part about not being able to imagine that anyone else could find him attractive.

I felt totally totally sick about not being there for Amy when she needed me. I tried to make up for it. I stayed by her side every day for the next week, listened when she needed to cry, and invited her to sleep over on the nights her mom and sister were out, so she didn't have to be alone. But still, every time I thought of her at that party, trying to get through to me, I felt this little stab of guilt somewhere in the vicinity of my heart.

× × ×

C.J. and I had a big talk soon after the Amy incident. Actually, I did most of the talking. I told him I was tired of having everything revolve around his skating life. "Can't we just, once in a while, do something that isn't skating-related? Like go to San Francisco or something? Just the two of us?"

I was thrilled when, a couple days later, C.J. suggested we go to the city that weekend. He planned a whole romantic day for us. First, we hiked across the Golden Gate Bridge, something I'd wanted to do since moving here. You can see all of San Francisco in front of you, and beyond that to Berkeley. Then we wound our way over to North Beach, the Italian part of town, where we had a delicious lunch at a restaurant C.J.'s parents always used to go to when they were dating. His dad had called ahead and spoken to the maître d', who treated us like celebrities. He seated us at a great table in the window, which was perfect for people-watching. And the waiters brought us all this extra food: little plates of homemade ravioli, stuffed mushrooms, gigantic prawns in garlic butter, plus a taste of every dessert on the menu.

In the middle of our meal, a lady came in with a basket of single red roses for sale, and C.J. bought the whole basket. So as we walked across the city hand in hand, I carried twenty long-stemmed roses.

And you're thinking: This is a bad thing? This amazingly romantic stroll through the city by the bay? The place that guy left his heart?

So yeah, our day in San Francisco was great.

Until. (You knew there had to be an until, didn't you?)

Until we just happened to walk by an office plaza where there just happened to be a couple of guys C.J. knew from skating taking advantage of the weekend emptiness to sail down the handrails and around the little walls. And well, we couldn't just walk by without stopping to say hi at least, could we? And how could C.J. refuse when one of them asked him for pointers?

And so, after our amazingly romantic date, I spent almost two hours (one hour and forty-three minutes, to be exact) sitting on a bench, watching. And waiting.

Here's the thing: Later that night, after we'd finally gotten back to Berkeley and C.J. had dropped me off at home, I found myself leaving the two hours on the bench watching and waiting out of my answer to Mim's "So, tell me all about it."

While she searched her cabinet for a vase big enough for the twenty roses, I told her all about the walk across the bridge and the food we'd tried and how nice they'd been at the restaurant and what fun it had been to people-watch our way through North Beach, and when she said, "Who knew C.J. could be such a romantic?" I just said, "Yeah," and smiled.

And I did the same thing when Amy came over later that night. I told her all the good stuff and left out all the bad.

But leaving out the bad didn't help at all as far as my own head went. It only made it worse. Because I knew what I was doing even as I did it. I knew that if I told Mim or Amy about how we just happened to bump into some skating buddies and how C.J. spent almost two hours of our so-called date skating, they'd say something like, "I thought this was supposed to be *your* special time?" (Mim) or "He skated for two hours in the middle of your date? And you just sat there?" (Amy).

× × ×

The third incident was much less dramatic. Hardly an incident at all, really. But coming as it did after the first two incidents, this one sent me over the edge, broke the camel's back, and all that, etcetera.

C.J. asked me to walk to the store and buy him a Red Bull.

That sounds innocent enough. He said "please" and he even called me "babe." But the thing is, he'd never asked me to wait on him like that before.

The second C.J. said, "Babe, would you please run over to 7-Eleven and get me a Red Bull?" while handing me a five-dollar bill, I realized that in C.J.'s eyes, I wasn't all that different from the Fan Club Girls I used to sneer at.

I was just a Fan Club Girl with benefits.

I took C.J.'s five, walked the block to the 7-Eleven, bought him his precious Red Bull, walked back, handed it over, and walked out of the skatepark for the last time.

Which sounds very *You go, girl,* and it would have been, if C.J. had even noticed. He just mumbled "Thanks" and continued watching Flip on the vert.

I had to spell it out for him later when he showed up at my house that night, as if nothing had happened, expecting me to go with him up to our spot on Grizzly. Which, yes, I did. I figured it would be way easier to talk there than in the living room with Mim and Leonard a room away.

It was the night before I was heading East for a vacation with Josh and my dad on Cape Cod, and it seemed as good a time as any. Breaking up then would leave us both free for whatever might come up over the summer. It would give us time to grieve or whatever and be emotionally fresh by the time the new school year started.

But C.J. simply could not get his head around the idea that I would break up with him. That anyone would break up with him. He'd always been the one to end it with previous girlfriends, and there had even been a little stalking situation with one of the exes. Plus, there were the Fan Club Girls and the online sluts.

So really, who can blame him for being totally, truly baffled when I told him I just didn't think it was working out anymore?

"We have a good time, don't we?" he asked, staring out over his steering wheel into the lights of San Francisco.

"Yeah," I said.

"And we've got chemistry," he said, reaching his hand out to the back of my neck. He grabbed my hair and pulled, as he had so many times over the last year.

I took a deep breath and didn't say anything as he

twisted my hair up and around, and let it fall. He leaned over and kissed me, and even though I was determined to break up, I kissed him back.

And then some.

And on the night I broke up with him, C.J. and I went further than we had ever gone, and it was more intense than it had ever been, and it was all I could do to resist the ultimate.

Why? Because it felt good. And I knew that it might be a long time before I'd be kissed and touched like that again.

But after we'd pulled back from that almost place, I made myself think about all those times I'd sat or stood on the sidelines while everyone *ooh*ed and *ah*ed over his acrobatics. About how he hadn't even looked at me that afternoon when I handed him his precious energy drink. And finally, how I'd betrayed my best friend—and lied about it—all so C.J. wouldn't have to stop kissing me while I took a phone call.

And I wouldn't kiss him again.

And he cried. Well, not right away. He tried a few more times, working the hair thing until I said, "Ow, C.J., stop. That hurts."

That's when his eyes filled with tears. Only one

actually made it onto his face. He wiped it away so quickly, it didn't have a chance to travel very far.

Then C.J. shut down. He wouldn't look at me or talk to me. He just started the pickup and drove me to my house and wouldn't respond when I tried to tell him how sorry I was and how much fun I'd had. He just glared out the windshield, looked at his watch, and flipped through his CD carrier. He said nothing when I said my final good-bye. And he didn't talk to me again.

× × ×

But he talked about me. Plenty.

12

Thou Shalt Not Dump the Skater Dude

CJLOGANLAND.COM

July 17

To all y'all who keep buggin me: Yeah, we broke up. Had to happen. The girl's a Total Sex Fiend. Never wanted to do anything else. I mean, come on, it's usually the girls who complain that we have only one thing on our minds . . . She cried when I told her. Which almost got to me, but I was strong. For those who might be interested in giving her a test-drive, keep in mind that the TSF goes from zero to sixty in no time flat, so operate with caution.

That's all I'm sayin.

× × ×

It's hard to say what was worse:

a.) The true parts,

b.) The made-up parts,

c.) Or the fact that I was reading this on the Internet and anyone who went to EBH would know he was talking about me. The alleged me.

Because—especially if you judged it by what went on that last night—it was true that things had gotten pretty hot between me and C.J.

But that night had been built up to slowly over the course of almost a year.

Before C.J., I hadn't done more than kiss. Well, not much more. I'd had a brief—as in one week—seventh-grade romance with an eighth-grader named Brian Thorne back in Boston, which involved a lot of kissing, some with tongue, and a brief moment of under-the-shirt, over-the-bra hand-to-breast contact. But that had done nothing for me except send me into hysterics, because it totally tickled, which totally embarrassed Brian, who never looked me in the face after that.

By the time C.J. came along I was ready to be touched—there and elsewhere. I enjoyed every moment in the front seat of his pickup all those nights. Plus that one night in the hot tub at my grandparents' when he and I got home before Mom and Mim and Leonard came back from the movies. And I'd enjoyed our last night together, even though I had known it was over.

C.J. had touched me in ways and places I'd never been touched before.

And yes, I liked it.

And he knew it. And he knew I didn't want to stop any more than he wanted to stop.

So I guess it really was true, in a way, that I couldn't "get enough." My body wanted more than my head was ready for, and I never pretended otherwise.

But the thing is, we always stopped. Sometimes I was the one to say, "We'd better stop." Sometimes it was C.J. Sometimes he had to get out of the truck and walk around taking deep breaths, but we always stopped.

It wasn't that I was all hung up on being a virgin until I turned some magic number or that I was saving myself for The One. I just wasn't ready in my head to cross the line my body wanted to cross. C.J. *said* he respected the fact that I didn't feel ready. One time he jokingly asked me if I thought I might feel ready anytime soon, but other than that, he didn't pressure me.

And up until that final night in his truck, getting hot and pulling back made us feel close. Or so I thought.

× × ×

I didn't discover C.J.'s online rampage until a couple of weeks after he posted it, after it had been sitting there, in view of the whole world. I'd gone to Cape Cod with Dad and Josh, and had a totally fun time at this weird hippie hotel retreat for single parents. I'd met a nice guy there, and we had kissed some and done the holding-hands-while-walking-on-the-beach thing. And I hadn't felt the least bit guilty about it, because I had been completely clear with C.J. and so I was a free agent.

When we got back to Dad's place in Boston, I went online to catch up with e-mail and to IM my new friends Tracy and Beka, whom I'd met at the Cape. Just out of curiosity, I went to C.J.'s blog. Silly me—I was worried about him. He'd seemed so hurt on our last night, I wanted to make sure he was okay. I wanted to see if he was back to his old, skating-obsessed self.

Apparently, he'd discovered a whole new self. A mean, lying, full-of-himself self.

I called Amy.

"Where are you?"

"At the Hut." Java Hut was a café near the U.C. campus where Amy and I would bring our laptops to use their wireless Internet.

"Are you online?"

"Yeah. . . ."

"Go to C.J.'s blog."

"What? Why? I thought you were over him."

"I am. I'm totally over him."

"Okay, and you're reading his blog because . . . ?"

"Please? Would you just please go to cjlogan-land.com?"

"Okay, okay. . . ." I heard the tapping of her key-board, then quiet and then, "Oh. Oh. Oh no. What a jerk."

"Why would he do that?"

"Um . . . maybe because he's totally in love with you and can't deal with the fact that you dumped him?"

"Oh please."

"Think about it. No one's ever dumped C.J. Logan. You've, like, broken a commandment or something. 'Thou shalt not dump the Skater Dude.' What we have here is a classic lashing-out scenario. He's hurt and so he's hurting you back."

Amy got quiet again. "Oh no."

"What?"

"Oh this is not good."

"What!?"

"Have you read the comments?"

Added by urgrl

Friday, August 5, 7:33 PM

what a skank! IM me cj—I can make u feel better.
<3 (let me be) urgrl

Added by q_t_lizzee

Thursday, July 28, 3:13 PM

cj u r better off without the TSF. I saw u skate in Sacto last weekend. I wuz in the white tank top with a butterfly tattoo you smiled & waved. Pls call me my frend has a car. Luv Lizzie xxx-xxx-xxxx

(Note from Kelsey: As stupid and mean as these girls obviously are, I'm not going to stoop to publishing their AIM IDs or phone numbers. That would be wrong. Fun maybe, but wrong.)

Added by sk8fan

Tuesday, July 19, 5:11 PM

I know a girl like that!!!!!She gave my boyfriend (and now me 2!) warts gross SKANK is rite

I clicked ADD A COMMENT and typed as fast as I could with one hand:

This is all a lie. I broke up with C.J.! He's making this all

up because he can't accept the fact that a girl would actually dump him. You are all so pathetic and by the way, don't you know that you're not supposed to post your phone number on the Internet? There are pervs on the lookout for girls like you—
TSF(not!)herself

Amy said, "What are you doing?"

"I can't let him get away with these lies." I read her what I wrote.

"And exactly who do you think will believe you?"

"I've got to defend myself." I moved my cursor over the POST button.

"Okay, Kelsey? Stop. Think. Think about what you're about to do."

"I can't let those lies sit out there like that. I have to defend myself."

"And what do you think's going to happen after your post? They'll all just say, 'Oh, okay, I didn't realize, but now that you explain it, I see that C.J. must be saying these things because of his bruised ego.' No. They—or C.J. himself—are going to attack back and it'll—"

"Amy?"

"Yeah?"

"It's too late."

"You posted?"

"Yup."

She just sighed. A very big sigh.

× × ×

Within two hours, C.J. had written a response to my comment, and this time, it didn't have *any* basis in reality. He said:

a.) That I'd been calling and IMing him all summer,

b.) That he'd had to change his cell phone number and screen name, and

c.) That he was thinking about getting a restraining order to protect himself. From me!

× × ×

If I'd only listened to Amy, I might have had a shred of dignity left at the beginning of sophomore year.

PART

xxx

TWO

13

Starting Over? Overrated.

Next to her place at the table in the breakfast nook, my grandmother has a shelf of inspirational books with titles like *Each Day a New Beginning*; *Zen Mind, Beginner's Mind*; *Starting Here, Starting Now;* and *Starting Over (Again!) at Sixty*.

I wasn't even sixteen yet, and I felt like I'd started over (again!) enough to last a lifetime.

In three years, I'd moved across the country, changed schools twice, gone from eighth-grade outcast to girlfriend of a superstar skateboarder to alleged skank reject of the alleged superstar.

I was tired of starting over. Starting over is overrated.

× × ×

But Amy insisted I do just that. Two weeks till school started, she called a meeting, the agenda of which was to construct a plan to Restore Our Dignity. Amy was the self-appointed motivational speaker. I was the unmotivated participant.

I didn't tell Amy about a phone call I'd made that morning.

"Scholastic Academy Admissions, how may I direct your call?"

"Um, yes, good morning," I said, in my best imitation-adult voice. "I'm calling to inquire about—"

"Applications for next year will be available in November. If you'd like to leave your address, we'll send them out to you as soon as they are available."

"Yes. Well. Umm, I'm calling to inquire about the possibilities of enrolling this year."

"For *this* term?" I swear I heard her laugh. Which, even if I was asking a totally ridiculous question, I thought was totally unprofessional.

"Yes, well, it's sort of a, um, special circumstance." I'd practiced and practiced, but the ums kept slipping out. "I'm calling on behalf of a well-known person in the, um, film industry whose identity I'm not at liberty to reveal at this moment."

"Yes." The receptionist sounded like she had a mile-long to-do list.

"Yes, well, um, this person, whose identity I'm—"

"Not at liberty to reveal—"

"Yes. Um, this person will be relocating to the Bay Area. This person has, um, had it with the dog-eat-dog world of Hollywood and wishes to raise her—or his—children away from the craziness of the dog-eat-dog world. Um . . ." I looked at my notes. I'd written out a whole story, loosely based on an article I'd read in *People* about an actress who had moved to Montana to raise her children away from the glare of Hollywood. My fictitious unnamed someone had a high school–aged child—a brilliant, high school–aged child. This certain unnamed someone, who had heard great things about the Scholastic curriculum, could also probably be counted on to make a sizable donation to the school's endowment sometime in the future.

Basically, I was just trying to figure out whether it was possible to buy your way into Scholastic. I'd figure out how to convince my dad to do it for me later.

"Our waiting list has twenty-five highly qualified students ahead of you. I mean, of the child of the very important person you represent. And while there are sometimes last-minute openings, and we do sometimes go as far down as number five or six, I'd say the chances of a September placement, even for the child of, say, Steven Spielberg, would be, well, zero."

"I see," I said, trying to maintain the dignity of my false identity. "Thank you very much; we'll just have to take our sizable donations elsewhere." But by then the line had gone dead.

× × ×

"Maybe we should try homeschooling. I bet Leonard would teach us. He's just gone from being semi- to all-the-way retired, and Mim's all worried that he's not going to have enough to do. This could be a real win-win."

Amy looked at me and drew a deep breath in through her nose. We both knew that this Restore-*Our*-Dignity thing was fiction. Amy's dignity was in fine shape. At drama camp, she'd met a new Retro-Punk-*Fully*-Vegan Drama Nerd who, unfortunately, lived in Seattle, but who had helped her get completely over Gabe.

After the humiliation of the *Crucible* cast party, she swore she'd never be able to show her face in the EBH theater again. But she'd gotten way over that and was practicing for next week's *Footloose* auditions.

"Kelsey, you've got to change your attitude. Remember how excited you were about going to

EBH a year ago, before C.J.? Hah, that's funny. B.C.J. like B.C.?"

"Hah. Hah hah. Hah hah hah hah hah."

"Oh, come on. I can't believe you're letting this guy get to you. You're acting like he really did dump you, as if you really are the pathetic girl of his pathetic dream-lies."

"Well, does it matter? I mean, if that's what everyone believes, what does it matter if it's not true? I'm sorry, but I just don't know how I'm going to get through this year."

Amy sighed again. She put a hand on her hip and held out the thumb of her other hand. "A. of all? It matters because it's not true. You are not that pathetic girl. And B. of all?" Her pointer finger popped out. "I'm sorry to say this, but you don't really think that people are going around thinking about you and C.J. Logan, do you?"

"Well . . ."

"I mean, sure, some people were probably buzzing about it a couple months ago when he first wrote all that crap. And, unfortunately, again when you posted your little comment. But it's history now. People have their own dramas. Believe me, they are not walking around obsessing about yours. What you need, my friend, is to throw yourself into something new. You want dignity? You've gotta act dignified. If you skulk around school, it's only going to make things worse. People are going to think you really are what C.J. said you were. Now, how about joining Drama Club?"

I thought about my terrible acting job on the phone that morning. "I can*not* act."

"You could work on sets or costumes or props."

I shook my head.

"Well, you've got to do something. You can't just spend the next year being C.J. Logan's Ex-Girlfriend. Now *that* would be truly pathetic."

Amy wasn't telling me anything I didn't know: I needed to establish myself as my own person. I needed to let people know the real me.

The thing was, though, I didn't know what "the real me" meant.

Being C.J. Logan's Girlfriend had allowed me to avoid all the big Who Am I?s you're supposed to ask yourself in high school. Before meeting him, I had been so excited about exploring new possibilities at East Bay High and becoming part of its huge, multicultural world. Other than that little yearbook page, the only extracurricular activity I'd engaged in was standing around the courtyard listening to

Skater Dudes. Sure, they had a language of their own, but you can't exactly call that multicultural.

"Okay," I told Amy. "You're right. I will throw myself into something. I was actually already kind of toying with an idea."

"Good. What is it?"

"I was thinking maybe of going out for the newspaper."

Amy's eyes widened. "*The Bee*?"

"Yeah. What?"

"Nothing."

"What?"

"Nothing. It's just—"

"What!?"

"Kelsey, *Bee* people are intense."

"This from a Drama Nerd? As if anyone could be more intense than the 'People of the Stage.'" I held the back of my hand to my forehead and fell back against the bare mattress on Ruth's bed.

But I knew what Amy was talking about. *The Bee* is run by the superachievers of East Bay High, the kids with all AP and Honors classes, the kids who take advanced science up at the university after they blaze through everything our school has to offer.

Mr. Rundle's the faculty advisor, and his classroom is right next to its office. I used to see last year's staff all the time. They seemed to spend every free moment of their lives working on the paper. Sometimes, Mr. Rundle told us, they'd work past midnight to make their deadline. But it seemed like they were having fun. There was always a lot of laughing coming from that room.

On the last day of school the year before, Mr. Rundle had the outgoing editors come and talk to our class about joining the paper. "You'll learn more doing that than I could ever teach you," he'd said.

And on my way out the door that day, Mr. Rundle had come up to me and said he hoped I'd seriously consider joining *The Bee*. He thought I'd make a good reporter since I asked a lot of questions in his class. At the time, I didn't even give it a second thought. My mind was too busy deciding whether or not to break up with C.J.

But as the first day of school drew closer and I tried to imagine how I was going to survive sophomore year, I remembered Mr. Rundle's suggestion.

Amy was scaring me.

"Maybe you're right. Maybe I should go back to yearbook. They're always desperate."

"No. No. Forget I said anything. You're right. I'm sorry. This is good. This is great. I don't know why I didn't think of it. I mean, you're always asking questions. You're not shy. You'd make a great reporter. You need something all-consuming to get your mind off the Skater Dude. This could be good. This could be very good."

"Really? You don't think I'll be in over my head?"

"No. No. I think you will rock as a reporter. There's just one thing."

"What?" I sat back up.

"Have you ever *met* Joanna Breslin?"

"No, who's Joanna Breslin?"

"She's the new editor, and she's scary."

"You know, for a motivational speaker, you're not exactly being motivational."

"Forget I said anything. I'm sure you'll do fine. I mean, you hung with the Skater Dudes for a year, right? And if they're not scary, I don't know who is. You'll do fine. Better than fine. Way better."

"Okay, okay, you can stop. I'm motivated."

14

My Reputation, and Other Exaggerations

On the first day of school, Mr. Rundle found me sitting in front of his trailer waiting for Amy, who'd promised to meet me back there before the bell rang. I couldn't yet bring myself to walk through the front door, across the lobby, and into the courtyard—a.k.a. C.J. territory—so I'd walked onto campus through the Trailer Park. Plus, I wanted to talk over the newspaper thing with Mr. Rundle.

x x x

"Amy says *Bee* people are scary." I plopped myself down at one of the student desks in the front row of his empty classroom. Mr. Rundle was reading through a file folder on his desk.

"Oh, don't believe the hype," he said. "The reputation of *The Bee* is greatly exaggerated."

"Like mine."

"What?"

I told Mr. Rundle about how C.J. trashed me online. He must have heard a lot of stories over the years, because he didn't seem exactly shocked.

"You mean you didn't hear about it?"

"Do you really think I spend my summer vacation reading high-school blogs?"

I shrugged. "I don't know, maybe. If you missed us you might."

He laughed. And I wasn't even making a joke that time.

"Okay. Enough about love. Let's talk career. Going out for *The Bee* is perfect for you. You'll make a great reporter. You always want to know the story behind the story."

In Mr. Rundle's class the year before, it had gotten to be a joke how I was always the first person to ask a question. By June, he was ending his lectures with, "Are there any questions—Kelsey?"

Everyone would laugh, including me, and then I'd ask something like "Why would anyone do that?"

And he'd say, "Can you be a little more specific?"

And I'd say something like, "Romeo and Juliet's parents. Why are they so stupid?"

And he'd coach me along until we ended up with something like "What are the sources of animosity between the Montagues and the Capulets?"

Not that I go around saying stuff like "sources of animosity." I could always count on Mr. Rundle to raise the level of my questions a notch or two.

"Yeah, but I don't exactly have the vocabulary for it, remember?"

"Doesn't matter. You're always asking questions. That's much more important when it comes to reporting," he said.

He walked over to the door connecting his trailer with *The Bee* office and unlocked it. "Come on in and take a look around while I turn on the computers."

I glanced out the tiny, smudged window on the door to Mr. Rundle's room. Still no sign of Amy. So I pulled myself out of the desk and joined Mr. Rundle.

The first thing I noticed was the row of brand-new computers with huge, flat-screen monitors along the back of the room.

"Hey, how come they have all this equipment and you can't even get a working air conditioner?" The spring before, right when we were reading the sweaty, climactic courtroom scene of *To Kill a Mockingbird*, Mr. Rundle's air conditioner had hissed itself to death.

"Different budgets. *The Bee* gets outside funding and donations from some of the high-tech companies around here."

Except for the equipment, the room was like the rest of our school: shabby. Piles of old newspapers lined one side. The opposite wall was filled with a mishmash of framed photographs containing yellowed news clippings. I walked over to get a better look.

In one picture, a smiling, tuxedoed guy stood between a smiling Bill Clinton and a smiling Stevie Wonder, both also in tuxes. Scribbled along the bottom was, "Hey kids, I started where you are now!" and a totally illegible signature. Another was of a woman dressed all in khaki, interviewing soldiers in the desert. Next to that was a copy of her yearbook profile from the eighties. She'd been editor in chief of *The Bee*, head of debate, a member of Alliance Française and Homecoming Queen.

"Mr. Rundle, forget it. I am so not *The Bee* type," I said.

"Oh, come on. There is no one type." As he talked, the door to his classroom opened and closed, rattling the walls and floor. Those portable classrooms sure were flimsy; I could hear every step the door opener took, crossing Mr. Rundle's classroom. "Journalism is very equal-opportunity," Mr. Rundle continued. "You're only as good as your last story."

"You are so right, Rundle-man." The tall, brown-haired source of the footsteps stood in the doorway.

"Well, if it isn't the editor in chief himself, returned from his adventures abroad." Mr. Rundle walked over to the doors between the rooms and offered his hand to Nathan Wexler. I'd never actually met Nathan, but I knew who he was. I'd seen him at some parties I'd gone to with C.J. He was supposed to be supersmart.

"*Co*-editor in chief," said Nathan, as he shook Mr. Rundle's hand and glanced over at me. "Don't let Joanna hear you calling me chief."

Mr. Rundle slapped his forehead in an exaggerated way and smiled. "Oh, man. You're right. I'd better watch myself. What was I thinking when I agreed to let you guys do this together?"

Nathan looked back at Mr. Rundle. "It's going to be fine, Rundle-man. We talked last night, and it's totally civil. We'll be fine."

"I hope so," said Mr. Rundle. He turned and held a hand out toward me. "I was just doing a little recruiting for you. Kelsey here is thinking about going out for reporter. She's got all the right instincts."

"Cool," said Nathan. "You look familiar—do I know you?"

That didn't used to be such a complicated question. Had he read C.J.'s lies? "I don't think so," I said, and felt myself blush.

It's weird, because if I try to describe Nathan part by part, he won't sound all that attractive. His quite curly hair sort of hung in his eyes and then dropped down to just below his ears. It was clean but not brushed, and a little clump stuck up on the top. His khakis were rumpled, and his T-shirt looked like it was one wash away from the rag pile.

But there was something in the overall effect of Nathan Wexler that was undeniably sexy. Of course it didn't hurt that his pants were belted right at the hips, so that just an inch or so of red-and-blue-plaid boxers showed when he moved his arm, like when he reached out to offer me his hand.

"So you're thinking about coming out for the paper?"

"Well, I—" I was kind of surprised to find myself checking Nathan out like that. After being burned by C.J., I'd decided to take a vow of celibacy for sophomore year. I hadn't even gone to my first class, and already I was thinking about breaking it. Maybe I really was a TSF.

"Cool," said Nathan, waking me up from my daydream. Then he turned and headed toward the computers at the back of the room. "Come to the meeting this afternoon." He sat down in front of a computer and reached for the mouse. The giant flat-screen burst into blue.

"Okay, bye," I said to the back of Nathan's head.

He lifted his hand from the mouse and gave me a backward wave. "See you this afternoon."

"Okay. Um. Maybe."

15

HARSH

The first half of my first day as C.J. Logan's *Ex*-Girlfriend, a.k.a. the Total Sex Fiend, wasn't as bad as I expected.

Nobody stared. Nobody pointed. Nobody walked by whispering "TSF" under their breath as I'd imagined, tossing and turning in my bed the night before.

Mostly they ignored me.

"See?" Amy said when we met up at my locker after our first two classes. "I told you people weren't going to be tripping about you and C.J. They've got their own lives."

And then it started. Third period had just ended. Amy had drama class way out in the Art Pavilion next, and it was impossible for us to meet up during the break and still get to our classes on time. So to avoid having to make eye contact with anyone, I went back to my locker to look busy. As I stood there, pretending to be deeply absorbed by my new schedule, I heard someone behind me say, "'Sup, beautiful?" I turned around to find myself face-to-face with Ryan Stansfield. Ryan was a sophomore I sort of knew. He'd been in my English class with Mr. Rundle and my French class last year.

"Oh. Hey, Ryan."

"Hey, girl. You lookin' goooood." He ran his eyes down to my feet and then back up, pausing for an excruciatingly long moment at chest level.

"Thanks." I guess.

"Long time no see, how's 'bout a hug?"

I slammed my locker shut and managed to step out of the way just as Ryan's arms closed in. On themselves.

"I'm late for history," I said, holding my schedule out and taking a step backward.

"Yeah? Who you got?" asked Ryan, taking a step forward.

"Umm. Baker," I said, attempting to turn and walk up the hall.

"Me, too. American history, Mr. Baker. Wait up,

girl, I'll walk witch you." He caught a corner of my messenger bag, pulled me back next to him, and put an arm around me. With his other hand, he hoisted up his ultrabaggies.

Okay. Here's some background information you need to picture this scene:

a.) Ryan is white. Like, you-can-see-his-veins-through-his-skin white.

b.) His family lives in the same part of town as mine, which isn't exactly the 'hood.

c.) When he had talked in Mr. Rundle's class the year before, which wasn't very often because he was allegedly shy, he wudn't talkin' no Ebonics, neither.

Apparently Ryan had undergone a radical personal style makeover and, for some reason, had decided to test it out on me. And why not? I mean, who better to try out your new playa moves on than the girl everyone knows is a Total Sex Fiend? Right?

"So, what else you takin' this semester?"

Seeing as escape seemed impossible, I started babbling to protect myself from any more moves. I told Ryan my whole schedule, trying to maintain a light, friendly, and totally un-sex-fiendish tone.

"Dat's cool, dat's cool," he said, splaying his fingers a bit for emphasis.

"And I'm going to check out *The Bee*." I don't know why I told him that part, except it was like I couldn't stop talking.

"Yeah?"

"Yeah. Remember when those editors came to our class at the end of last year?"

"Yeah . . . yeah." Ryan nodded. "You know, I was thinking 'bout that, too. Givin' it some real thought. When's it meet?"

"Mondays and Wednesdays, seventh period."

He nodded. "Yeah? Today's Wednesday. Where's it at?"

"The trailer next to Mr. Rundle's."

"Yeah? Cool. I'ma think 'bout th—dat. Check it out. Thanks for the suggestion."

The suggestion? Before I could say anything back, I practically bumped into Mr. Baker, who was standing just inside the doorway to his room wearing a red-white-and-blue-striped bow tie, holding a clipboard with a seating chart. Mr. Baker was famous at EBH for wearing bow ties and running one of the strictest classrooms.

"Good morning. May I have your names, please?"

"Stans—"

Mr. Baker held a hand up to interrupt Ryan.

"Ladies first. Ladies first." He turned to me. "Miss?"

"Wilcox. I'm Kelsey Wilcox."

Mr. Baker looked down at his seating chart. "Wilcox, Wilcox . . . There you are. You're in the front row here, next to Miss Alteri." He nodded over to an empty desk, next to which sat Kiki Alteri.

Kiki Alteri was S-Man's girlfriend, and she and I had stood around together, waiting and watching at various skating competitions all last year. We'd even ridden BART—that's our subway—home together a couple of times when the guys' events had gone on past dark.

You'd think she'd never seen me before in her life by the way she looked at me when I sat down next to her. Or didn't look at me is more like it. She sort of stole a little glance and then pretended to be totally absorbed in doodling on her notebook.

"Hi, Kiki."

She did one of those totally fake, oh-I-didn't-recognize-you "hiiiiieeee"s back.

"How was your summer?" I asked.

"Fine." She gave me half a smile and went on doodling.

I fingered my phone. If Mr. Baker had just let me sit at the back, I could be text messaging Amy for moral support. Instead, I had to sit there smiling, pretending I cared about his introductory lecture on the philosophical roots of the American Revolution and pretending I didn't care about people like Kiki, who did everything she could to avoid looking at me, or people like Ryan, who wouldn't stop looking.

× × ×

The big test came at lunchtime, when I had to cross the courtyard. The first person I saw was Julie Miller, Flip's girlfriend. Like Kiki, she acted like she'd never seen me before.

"Hi, Julie," I said, mostly out of spite.

"Oh. Hi, Kelsey." She barely slowed down. Her eyes scanned the horizon for her escape.

"How was your summer?" I wasn't letting her off that easy.

"Oh, fine. I did a lot of traveling with Flip and . . ." She stopped and paused for dramatic effect. "The guys."

"Yeah? How is Flip?"

"Oh, you know—"

Totally boring and self-centered, like C.J.? Yeah, I know.

"Busy," she said. "He's thinking about going pro."

"Really? Wow." I widened my eyes as if I cared. How could I have spent an entire year talking to girls like this who don't know how to talk about anything but their boyfriends? How could I have spent an entire year *being* a girl like that?

"Yeah, well, nice seeing you, Kelsey. I'm really sorry to hear about you and C.J. He'll be sorry when he realizes what he's lost." She started to take a step.

"Julie." I touched her shoulder. "You know I broke up with C.J., right?"

She looked at me with pity. Like I was some poor delusional dumped girlfriend. "Oh? No, I didn't know that. Well, maybe it was for the best then. I'm going to miss seeing you at the contests. There's Flip—gotta go, Kelsey. You take care of yourself, okay?" She reached out and gave my hand a pity squeeze.

Flip was standing next to C.J.

Seeing him made me feel totally weird. It was the first time I'd laid eyes on him since the night I'd broken things off. Part of me went all nostalgic and got warm and tingly thinking about how, if we were still together, I'd walk over to him and he'd put his arm around me, maybe nuzzle me on the neck or brush his lips against my ear. And for a second—just a teeny, tiny second—I had this over-before-it-started feeling of regret. Life had been so much easier as C.J. Logan's Girlfriend.

He didn't even look at me, but I knew he knew I was walking by, because Flip had seen me and Julie talking. He had leaned over and whispered something into C.J.'s ear. C.J. nodded and kept his eyes straight ahead. But I could tell that he was concentrating on not looking in my direction. Plus his voice grew louder and louder the closer I got, talking about some jump he'd seen somebody take.

Hey, look at me, I'm still cool; everybody listens when C.J. Logan talks.

I walked as fast as I could through the crowded courtyard, wishing I could fly, wishing I could breaststroke my way into the air like in my dreams and float down to meet Amy at our designated meeting spot out back in the Trailer Park.

But there was no way to avoid those junior and senior girls who used to pretend to care about me when I was part of the magic C.J. circle. They looked right at me now, making no attempt to hide their smirks.

× × ×

I found Amy sitting on the concrete wall overlooking the faculty parking lot talking on the phone.

"Ruth," she mouthed. Then, back into the phone, she said, "Ouch. Yeah, well—I'd be bitter, too. Uh-huh. Oh. That's weird."

Earlier that morning when I'd told Amy about meeting Nathan, and the conversation he and Mr. Rundle had had about Joanna, she put in an emergency information-gathering call to Ruth at UCLA. Ruth had to check in with someone named Katie, who'd been on *The Bee* staff the year before and now went to NYU. Apparently, Katie would have the low-down on the Nathan-Joanna situation.

"Okay. Okay. Yeah, well we put your bed out on the sidewalk this weekend with a FREE sign. You wouldn't believe how fast it went. It's so roomy now. I love it. . . . On the trundle. . . . Oh, come on. It isn't *our* room anymore, sister dear, it's mine. . . . Oh, I'm supposed to let all that space go to waste while you're living large in L.A.?"

I tugged on Amy's T-shirt. "I gotta go," she said. "Yeah, I do. The bell just rang. . . ." Amy flipped her phone closed. "God is she a control freak! Can you believe she expected me to just leave the room like it was?"

"Sorta."

Amy looked at me.

"I mean, not that you should leave the room as

she left it. But I don't know that you had to rub it in with that bit about putting her bed out on the sidewalk. You didn't really do that, did you?"

"Yeah we did."

"You did not."

"Seriously. We did. My mom didn't want to deal with calling the Salvation Army. So we put it out on the sidewalk. It was move-in day, and the Cal students were out scrounging. It was gone in a half hour."

"That's harsh."

Amy shrugged. "You know what's harsh?"

"What?"

"Breaking up with your girlfriend of three years by e-mail. From Italy. Because you met some Italian contessa or something."

"Nathan did that? Yikes. He seemed so nice."

"Yeah, well. According to Ruth, who got it from Katie, who used to go out with Joanna's older brother, their relationship was already sort of a dying animal. But she thought they'd ride it out till graduation. Why do people do that? So then Nathan went to Italy this summer on some exchange program and supposedly fell in love with an Italian heiress or princess or model or something, and he sent Joanna an e-mail saying he wanted to break up. I guess so he could have a guilt-free fling."

"Ouch."

"Yeah. And so the crazy thing is, he and Joanna are now co-editors of the paper. Last year, when everything was status quo, they didn't want to run against each other and make all their mutual newspaper friends choose between them in an election, and so they just decided to run as a joint ticket. Ruth says that Joanna was already a scary individual before the Nathan e-mail breakup. She advises against joining *The Bee*."

16

It's All About the Questions

Joanna didn't look scary.

"Good afternoon, cubbies," she said, walking up to the whiteboard and turning her back to us. New staff members were known as "cub reporters." At first, I thought it was cute the way the editors called us cubbies. It didn't take too long, though, for me to realize that cubby was synonymous with peon.

Joanna had long, straight brown hair, which she wore loose, and which she must have just brushed because it was all shiny and perfect. The hair fell just below her shoulders, which were peeking out of a sheer, dark green hippie-ish shirt. Her jeans were vintage Levi's, the ones with the red label on the pocket, and they were well worn without being the least bit raggedy.

She seemed nice enough.

Until I saw her in action.

She grabbed the one marker that was sitting in the rack below the board, pulled the top off with her teeth, and tried to write, but the marker was so dry that nothing showed up on the board.

"Didn't I tell someone to order markers?!" She pulled a Palm Pilot out of her pocket, made a few taps with her stylus, and said, "Lizzie!? Where is Lizzie?"

"Orthodontist," said Nathan, without actually looking up from the laptop in front of him. He'd been sitting there, tapping away while Joanna talked. Or rather, yelled.

"Damn it," said Joanna. She stuck the little nub on the end of the marker in her mouth and winced. Then she turned to the board and wrote FACTS in fat-but-faint green letters on one side, and QUESTIONS on the other.

She turned back to us and started pacing. "Reporting is all about learning to ask questions. Good reporters think outside the parameters of their circumscribed lives."

Bee editors, I would soon learn, throw SAT words like "parameter" and "circumscribed" around all the time, especially when they're talking to cubs.

For the next fifteen minutes, all the wannabe *Bee* reporters were lectured about the role of facts and questions in reporting, which can basically be summed up by the phrase, "It's all about the questions, cubbies," which Joanna must have said fifty times.

I spent most of the time studying the cub handbook:

> *You will be credited with a byline if the story is responsibly written and submitted in* Bee *style. If your editor must make major revisions, the byline will be dropped. In some cases, if your editor or another reporter does substantial additional research or rewriting, he or she will receive the byline in lieu of the original writer. Cub reporters whose bylines appear ten times over the course of their cub year will be promoted to staff reporters and will be eligible to apply for editorial positions thereafter.*

× × ×

When Joanna wrapped up her little lecture, she sat down in a desk across the room from Nathan, folded her arms in front of her chest, and stared at him. I don't know if he was pretending to be too absorbed in what he was looking at to notice, or if he really was too absorbed to notice.

She waited a bit, and when he still hadn't budged, she said, "And now Nathan Wexler will explain how we do the first assignment."

Nathan finally looked up. "Oh, man, I'm sorry, I was in my own world there."

Joanna rolled her eyes and uncrossed and recrossed her arms.

Nathan bent over and dug around in his backpack, one of those army surplus jobs. He pulled out a pen and clipboard and sprinted to the front of the room.

"Hey, you made it," he said, nodding my way. I blushed.

"Uh, let's not waste any more time," Joanna said, looking at me, and then back at Nathan. "We've got to explain the Story Hunt."

Without looking at her, Nathan glanced at his clipboard. "Okay, cubs, now you are about to take part in a tradition that *Bee* reporters have been participating in since 1945. . . ."

Joanna stood up again, walked to the whiteboard, and talked as she wrote. "It's your chance to demonstrate the Three I's: Initiative, Ingenuity, and Imagination." She underlined the "I" in each word and half the room scribbled notes.

"Do you want to do this?" Now Nathan was

looking directly at Joanna, who stared back.

"No. I was just—"

"The Story Hunt, cubs, is your first test. It's about you going out into the world and looking at it with a reporter's eye. What captures your attention? What are the things people need to know about?"

Nathan explained that over the next two weeks we were supposed to "sniff out" and "hunt down" a story worthy of *The Bee*. It was supposed to be "fresh, original, and relevant" to the kids in our school. The best stories would be published in *The Bee* if they were "newsworthy" and "reported skillfully." But we weren't supposed to worry about publication just yet. The staff reporters who'd survived last year's grueling initiation and the editors would be putting out the first few issues.

"But right now, guys"—Nathan looked at me—"the object here is to learn, to develop your reporter's eye. To get your information and shape it into something coherent. Um, yeah, in the back there. You have a question?"

"Yo, I wanna do one a them, uh whaddya call it, when you ride along with the cops in the squad car?"

The voice was unmistakable. I turned around to see Ryan Stansfield at the back of the room, feet propped up on the seat of the empty desk next to him.

Nathan opened his mouth to answer, but Joanna beat him to it. "A ride-along. It's called a ride-along and forget it. Cubs can't do ride-alongs."

Nathan scowled at Joanna and then smiled at Ryan. "What she means is, we usually discourage cubs from taking on something that big for the Story Hunt."

Joanna cleared her throat. "What I mean is, forget it. What's your name?"

"Stansfield. Ryan Stansfield. I wanna do the crime beat."

"Yo, Ryan. Listen up. The cops let us do one ride-along with them a year. And yours truly, who has two years' seniority on you, is doing this year's ride-along. If you want the privilege—and it is a privilege, earned by showing you have the initiative, ingenuity, and imagination it takes to be a reporter—then maybe, maybe next year we'll consider—"

Nathan interrupted her. "Ryan, listen man, it's better to learn the basics with smaller stories. Look for things you encounter in your everyday life. Do you have any other ideas?"

"Yeah," he said, looking at Joanna. "Matter of fact, I do. You know how stores around here put up those lame-ass signs saying only two students can come in at a time? Isn't that, like, discriminationatory or something?"

"Um, no," said Joanna, not even bothering to look up from her Palm Pilot this time.

"Why not?" asked Ryan. Joanna ignored him while she scribbled into her Palm.

But when Nathan asked, "Yeah, why not?" she finally looked up.

"We did it," Joanna said to Nathan. "Don't you remember? Two years ago?" She turned to Ryan. "It's totally legal. They're allowed to discriminate against minors. We have no right to shop."

"Okay, but how about the way it's enforced, huh? Myself and these two friends a mine—they darker skinned'n me—got yelled at by this guy because we walked into Lee's Market together. He went apeshit, tellin' us, 'Read the sign! Read the sign! Two at a time! Two students at a time!' Like we was criminals. But three white girls walk in, three at a time, four at a time, the guy says, 'Hey,' all smiley and shit, 'how's it going? Can I help you?' It's totally discriminationatory."

At exactly the same time, Joanna barked "Nope," and Nathan said, "You might have something there."

Joanna turned to Nathan. "There's no hook, nothing new to report." Her nostrils had gotten wider; she was biting her top lip with her bottom teeth. The prettiness was gone.

Nathan ignored her and said to Ryan, "Let's talk about it some more, dude. See if we can come up with a fresh approach."

Joanna glared at Nathan. She slipped the stylus back into its slot on her Palm, closed it, and stomped out of the room.

Nathan looked to Mr. Rundle, who'd been quietly observing the whole thing from the back of the room, and shrugged.

Mr. Rundle said, "So good luck to all the cubs with the Story Hunt. Get in touch with us if you have questions, and we'll see you next meeting."

× × ×

"Man that Joanna's a hard-ass." Despite my efforts to slip away from the meeting as fast as I could, Ryan caught up with me as I crossed the Trailer Park. I was supposed to meet Amy outside the theater.

"Yeah, I might be rethinking this whole thing." Ruth was right. Joanna was scary.

" 'Cause a her? Nah, Kelsey, you gotta stay. You got me all stoked about bein' a reporter. You gots ta stick widdit."

"I did? I do?"

"Yeah, girl. You're the one who got me to check it out. Now you talkin' 'bout quittin' on me?"

"Um, Ryan?"

"Yo."

"Do you think you could talk normal? 'Cause I might consider staying on if you do—at least when you talk to me. I mean, doesn't it get tiring?"

17

BISTRO.TEKNO.TERIA, OR, HOW NOT TO RUN A RESTAURANT

When I told Mim I'd gone to *The Bee* meeting, she got all excited and said we should go out to dinner to celebrate.

I realize that probably seems like an overreaction.

But my joining the newspaper was just the excuse of the day. If I'd come home and said I'd successfully memorized my new locker combination, Mim would probably have wanted to celebrate that, too.

The celebration threshold in our house is low. It's been that way ever since Mim turned sixty and declared she was retiring from kitchen duty. It must have been one of those inspirational seize-the-day books. Leonard never bothered to learn how to cook, and my mom is always at the law library and always on a diet, anyway. We eat a lot of takeout and frozen pizza, and we're always trying new already prepared foods from the gourmet supermarket.

"Your father's flying in this afternoon," Mim said. "We'll go somewhere close to campus, so your mother can join us."

"We'll 'greet you at the beginning of a great career,' as Emerson did Whitman," Leonard, the newly retired English professor, piped in from his semipermanent position in his easy chair by the window, where he sat with his binoculars to his eyes, on the lookout for birds.

"Leonard, you always know just what to say." Mim beamed at him from across the room, where she was sorting mail.

"You guys? I only went to a meeting. I'm really not sure this newspaper thing's going to work out. The people in charge are a little nuts. And it's very competitive."

"A little competition never hurt anyone," said Leonard.

"Don't sell yourself short, honey," said Mim. "You never know unless you give it a try." Mim was full of inspirational sayings.

"Can we go to b.t.t.?" Josh asked from his semipermanent position in front of his Game Cube. Ever since it had opened downtown, he'd been nagging us about going to bistro.tekno.teria, "Berkeley's first all-wireless restaurant."

But so far he'd been unsuccessful. Leonard said he was against it on principle. "I won't eat in a place that uses periods in the middle of words and invents its own spelling. I just cannot abide these practices. And what the heck does that mean, 'first all-wireless restaurant'? Tell me that. Is there such a thing as a wire*full* restaurant?"

"Wired, Leonard. Wireless or *wired*." Josh went on to explain how you ordered through a computer touch screen that sent signals into a wireless receiver in the kitchen, to which Leonard just grunted.

Mim didn't want to go because she thought b.t.t. would be too crowded.

"The line's been out the door and around the block ever since it opened," she said as she stood before the organizers lining the kitchen wall. Mim has an organizer, a basket, a box, or a shelf for everything.

Josh had obviously prepared for this opportunity. "Not anymore," he said. "Adam went for his birthday last week and said they only had to wait fifteen minutes."

Mim looked over at Josh with a raised eyebrow. "Fifteen minutes?"

"Call Adam's mom," he said to Mim. "She'll tell you. It's really not as crowded anymore. Can't we please? Can't we? I hear it's so cool. You can build your own burgers—and pasta, Mim, I hear they have great pasta—with a drag-and-click menu. So you can tell them exactly how you want things. You can even watch your food cooking through streaming video."

"Sounds like they reinvented the Automat," said Mim. "Remember when we used to go to the Automat, Leonard?" She tossed the last bit of junk mail into the recycling bin and headed over to Leonard's chair.

"Everything was always stale. The bread was crusty and the mayonnaise was yellow."

"That is not true," she said as she perched herself on her spot at the edge of the chair's arm. She sat there so much that the fabric had worn through to show the white stuffing underneath. "You loved the cheesecake and the lemon meringue pie. You used to stand there looking in every window for the biggest piece, so we could share. Even though they were always exactly the same size."

Leonard put his binoculars in his lap and looked up at the woman he'd been living with for, like, ever. He had that back-to-the-old-days look in his eye.

When that happened, Mim could convince him of anything.

× × ×

We caught up with Dad an hour later, at the end of the block-long line. He was working his cell phone, as usual. He held his index finger up to say, "Gimme a minute," which was never quite enough. He took me and Josh into a big bear hug, talking all the while.

"Yeah, hi, Larry Wilcox here, is Dan around?" he said into the phone. "Hi guys," he said to us. "This is the place to be, huh?" Then back into the phone. "Hey, Dan, you'll never guess where I am. . . . No, no. I'm standing in a line that's going down the block. . . . Uh-huh. . . . Nope. Give up? . . . Your new restaurant. . . . Yeah, b.t.t. in Berkeley. . . . Yeah, yeah, yeah. . . . Okay, thanks, bye." He clicked off and gave Mim and Leonard each a big hug.

"What did you do, Larry Wilcox?" Mim asked in the pretend scolding voice she took with Dad a lot.

"Nothing, Myra," he said as he planted a big kiss on her cheek. "Can't a guy call an old friend to congratulate him on the success of his new business venture?"

Just then, a woman in bright green cat's-eye glasses walked up, carrying a matching green Palm Pilot. "Mr. Wilcox?"

"That's me."

"Your table is ready."

Mom flew in the b.t.t. door according to plan, just as we were figuring out the menu.

She had just started her third year of law school and was still as anal about studying as ever. I hate that word, which Mim once tried to explain to me had something to do with Sigmund Freud's theory of human development. But it really suits my mom.

All her studying had paid off. Big time. She'd made *Law Review*, which is like this huge honor, but which also means you have to work even harder, putting out this big magazine-book thing with really long articles about complicated legal matters. So we were seeing even less of her during the week. Every once in a while, if we ate in a restaurant close enough to the law library, Mim could convince her to join us for dinner on a school night.

"Hi, Nan," said my dad, as he stood up and pulled a chair out for Mom.

"Hey, Lar." Mom offered him her cheek and let him push her chair into the table.

Josh took charge of the touch-screen menu

mounted on the wall above our table. Everyone kept shouting orders at him.

"Let me see the salads," said Mom.

"'Pub Grub,' that sounds good," said Dad. "Cheeseburger for me."

"What kind of cheese?" asked Josh, who was operating the drag-and-click.

"Do they have blue?"

Mom shuddered. "Blue cheese? Uck, Larry, your breath."

"Oh, and extra red onion on that, Joshy." Dad blew an exaggerated kiss across the table at Mom. Who pretended to get hit with a wave of bad breath.

× × ×

The other big news in our family was that Dad and Carolyn had broken off their engagement. She'd shown up one afternoon—unexpected and uninvited—at the place Dad had taken me and Josh on Cape Cod. The two of them disappeared for a seven-hour dinner. (I know because I watched out the window until he finally came back, alone, at one A.M.). In the morning, Dad told me and Josh they'd decided to postpone their wedding but it was only a matter of days before "postpone" turned into "call off," and by the time we got back from the Cape,

Carolyn had cleared all her stuff out of Dad's house. (Except for this one jar of expensive-looking "Nighttime Facial Renewal Cream" I found in the guest bathroom and made the mistake of trying one night. I woke up with pink, throbbing skin that peeled for days.)

Personally, I never understood what Dad saw in Carolyn. His explanation for the breakup was that they didn't have a "shared vision for their shared future." Mom said it meant Carolyn wanted to have kids and Dad didn't want any more and that she couldn't get behind the bicoastal lifestyle.

"So." I took a deep breath. We were at the gym side by side on elliptical trainers. "Are you two going to start, you know, dating or something now?"

"What? Me and your father?" You'd think I'd asked her if she was going to date her own father by the look on her face. "Kelsey, honey, are you still hoping we'll get back together?"

"No." In fact I'd been dreading that possibility. "But I thought you guys were sort of—"

"Friends. Your father and I have realized, after all this time, that we are really good friends. Our sexual connection is over." Mom increased the speed on her trainer.

Which was a bit more information than I'd needed at the moment, but it put my mind at ease about what was going on between them.

× × ×

Josh clicked to the pasta page and started to put together Mim's drag-and-click dinner.

"Linguine, fusilli, or penne?"

"It's so complicated." She squinted at the screen. "Which one's fusilli? Is that the spirals or the bow ties?"

"Spirals," grunted Leonard. Clearly, seeing the place for himself had not, as Josh promised, changed his mind.

Next Mim had to pick a sauce. Cream-based. Meat-based. Vegetarian. Vegan.

Leonard got so fed up waiting his turn to see the fish offerings, he called the manager over to ask if he could get a regular handheld menu.

"I'm sorry, Mr. Wilcox—"

"My name's not Wilcox, it's Sherman."

"I'm sorry, Mr. Sherman, b.t.t. is a wireless *and* paperless enterprise. That reflects our commitment to the environment."

"A slate board? How 'bout a good old-fashioned

slate board and chalk? All I want to know is what kind of fish you have."

"Oh, that's simple." The manager took one of those collapsible pointers that look like pens from his front pocket, extended it, and aimed at the screen. "To find our seafood offerings, you just click on the fish icon up there in the right corner. You'll get a scroll-down menu, allowing you to choose from the shellfish, ocean, and freshwater offerings. Each of our menu items . . ."

But Leonard wasn't listening.

"If I wanted to work this hard I'd have stayed home. Just order me a grilled salmon, Joshy. Everybody's got grilled salmon, right?"

"Sure, Leonard. It's right here."

Meanwhile, Mom's watch-checking had reached its usual, obsessive pace. She must have looked five times while we were ordering.

× × ×

"Turn it over, turn it over," Leonard said a few minutes later. He was staring at the computer monitor, watching the cook ruin his salmon, courtesy of b.t.t.'s streaming video. "If they don't flip that fish in the next thirty seconds it won't be any good." He looked to Mim.

"Turn that thing off, Josh, your grandfather's heart can't take it."

"But I just wanna see how they do this." Josh clicked something and a bunch of coding came up on the screen.

"Josh, turn it off; we'll all be happier. Thank you." She was bordering on yelling, and bordering on yelling was as mad as Mim got.

× × ×

When our food finally arrived, Mom took only a few bites of her grilled chicken Caesar salad before asking them to box it up. Then she headed back to the law library. Leonard took one bite of his salmon before announcing it was so dry, "I wouldn't even give it to my cat, if I had a cat."

Even Dad, who usually didn't care what he ate, said his burger tasted like a hockey puck. "Once the glow of the computer gimmick wears off, this place is history."

"They ought to forget all the computer stuff and learn something about food," Mim said, picking through her pasta, which she said was "no better than Kraft's Macaroni and Cheese."

× × ×

On our way back to Mim's Volvo, we came upon a group of street kids sitting in a circle, with a collection of food in the middle: restaurant take-out boxes, a garbage bag full of bagels, and the biggest bag filled with the biggest carrots I had ever seen. The bag had a picture of a cartoon bunny chomping a carrot under the words 100% ORGANIC.

There were also a couple of dogs, on leashes, with paper cups of water in front of them. Assorted backpacks leaned against the window of IN SYNC: YOUR SOURCE FOR CUSTOMIZED KITCHEN CABINETRY AND APPLIANCES.

"Good evening," one of the boys said, eyeing the white cardboard box Mim was carrying with the uneaten part of her fusilli. Why she had accepted the waiter's offer to box it up for her was a mystery.

"Good evening," Mim said, smiling, slowing down, and then stopping. A few paces ahead, the rest of us stopped to watch.

"Would you consider making a contribution to our evening meal, ma'am?"

"Well, I suppose I could. Just a moment," she said, starting to dig around in her gigantic purse.

Dad shook his head and rolled his eyes. Leonard shrugged a what-are-you-gonna-do?-that's-Mim shrug.

The boy pointed to her box of leftovers. "I meant that."

"This?" She shook her head. "I really don't think you want this. It's no better than Kraft's. Let me give you a few dollars and you can buy something better."

"Kraft's is good," said the boy.

"We love Kraft's," said another.

"It would make a nice addition to our buffet," said the first boy, gesturing at the food in the center of the circle. "A few dollars would be great, ma'am. Above and beyond what most people give us—"

"When they bother to give us anything," said the only girl in the group, who'd been completely quiet up to then. She was sitting off to the side, by herself. She had green hair, and very pale skin, and she was holding a puppy in her lap. She looked up at Mim and then over at me and Dad. Then she looked back down and whispered something to her puppy.

"But we'd appreciate the food even more," said the first boy, the one who'd started the whole conversation with Mim.

"Of course, of course," said Mim, holding the box out. "Here you are. . . . May I ask your name?"

"Jimmy."

"Hello, Jimmy. I'm Myra Sherman. Everyone—including my grandchildren here—calls me Mim."

"Myra, it's time to call it a night," said Leonard, looking at his watch. "We've got to get the kids to bed."

"Well, everyone except my husband, when he's annoyed with me." Mim opened her wallet, handed Jimmy what looked to me like more than "a few" dollars, plus one of her business cards, said good night, and scurried to join us.

× × ×

When we were far enough away from the kids, Dad lit into Mim. I'd never heard him talk to her like that.

"The food I don't have a problem with. But your business card? What were you thinking?"

"Larry, I'm a therapist; I know people who could help those kids."

"Is your address on that card, Mim?"

Mim sighed. Her office is in a cottage behind our house.

"Aw, geez," said Dad. "And exactly how much did you give him?"

Mim shrugged. "I didn't count, Larry. A few bucks. What's the big deal? I think you're overreacting." I thought of the time I'd seen Dad give that homeless woman sixty dollars.

"The only thing you are going to hear from that kid is, 'Lady, can I have some more money?' That's if you're lucky—if he doesn't come and demand it. Maybe we should tell the police."

"What are you talking about, Larry? Do you really think those kids are going to come to the house?"

"Maybe. Maybe. Mim, don't you know you're not supposed to give them money? That just encourages them."

"Encourages *them* to do *what*?"

"To stay on the street. There are plenty of programs to help kids like that."

"Are there, Larry?"

"Sure. There are soup kitchens and shelters and jobs programs—"

"And what exactly do you mean when you say 'kids like that'? What do you know about why that kid is on the street?"

"He probably doesn't like having to live by his parents' rules. Wants to smoke dope with his buddies. Skip school."

At this point, I felt like I had to jump in. "Oh come on, you don't know that, Dad. Maybe it's his parents who are the druggies. Maybe they kicked him out. Maybe they're dead." When I was with C.J., I'd met some kids whose lives were pretty rough, who'd left home to get away from bad situations.

We arrived at Mim's car. Dad's rental was another block up. He was spending the night at a hotel in San Francisco. He hadn't gotten around to buying—or even looking for—his own place out here.

"Now, now, let's agree to disagree, or whatever we're doing here," said Mim, opening her arms to hug Dad.

"Mim, you're an idealist. That's good. The world needs idealists to dream for us. Me, I'm a realist. I see things as they are."

"Larry, we're making up here, don't start with this realist-idealist crap if you don't want me to get all worked up again."

"Sorry, Mim," he said, hanging his head in pretend shame. "Sorry. Sorry."

She kissed him on the forehead.

x x x

On the way home, I stared out the window, thinking. I hated to hear Mim and Dad fight, but the fight had totally inspired me—professionally speaking.

18

ON THE STREET WITH NEWSGIRL

Saturday, I took a bus down to Telegraph Avenue with a camera in one hand and a microcassette recorder in the other.

I must have walked up and down the block across from where the street kids hung out ten times before I finally got up my nerve to cross. And even once I was within talking distance of the pierced, greasy-haired kids who sit on the sidewalk outside Rasputin's, this block-long record store, it took a while to get up my nerve to try talking to anyone.

Some of the kids sat behind handmade signs like SPARECHANGE.COM, PLEASE GIVE MONEY FOR FOOD, I'M HUNGRY, and THANK YOU FOR GIVING (GENEROUSLY). My favorite was I TRIED GETTING A JOB, BUT THEY WANTED ME TO WORK, SO I QUIT.

Something about it just made me laugh. I snuck a glance into some of the cups and cans next to these signs. None had more than a few coins.

But there were two guys—musicians—who, judging by the crowd gathered around them and the dollars piled up in the guitar case at their feet, seemed to be doing okay.

One kid was black, the other white. The black guy played an electric guitar that was connected to a tiny amp, which I guess ran on some kind of battery because it wasn't plugged into anything. The white guy had a little conga drum, but he didn't seem to be contributing much to the music. Mostly, his job was to watch people who were walking by and shout out a detail about their appearance. And then the guitar guy would make up a verse—on the spot—about the person walking by. For example:

A twenty-something woman in an expensive-looking suit, stockings, and heels approached. The look-out guy gave her the once-over and called out "purple shoes." They were a deep, sort of smoky purple sling-back with a very high heel. Very nice, and *very* unusual for Berkeley, especially Telegraph Avenue where tie-dye, hairy legs, and Birkenstocks rule.

On the spot, the guitar player sang, with a Carribean twang,

"Purple Shoes, Purple Shoes
Purple Shoes done paid her dues."

At this point, Purple Shoes slowed down to see what everyone was looking at. She peered over the sidewalk audience. I don't think she had any idea she was part of the act until the guitar player looked right at her and half said, half sang, "Hey there, Purple Shoes."

Ms. Purple Shoes took a quick look down at her feet and frowned. Everyone else laughed.

The guitar player sang on:

"Purple Shoes, Purple Shoes,
Purple Shoes done paid her dues.
Wonders why
I don't get a job. . . ."

After he sang that line, he looked at Ms. Purple Shoes and with a big smile sang,

"Purple Shoes tink dat I'm a slob—"

At that point, I started to wonder whether the accent was real.

Purple Shoes shook her head, turned, and

stomped off. Well, she couldn't really stomp in those heels, but she tried. And without missing a beat, the guy sang,

"I tink Purple Shoes is a snob."

The audience laughed and clapped.

Next came the chorus:

"Passersby
Pass us by,
Never stop
To wonder why
They are there
And we are here."

They ran through this a couple times while some of the audience moved on, many of them throwing a few coins or a dollar bill into the case.

And then Conga Guy called out, "Leather Jacket."

And Guitar Guy started,

"Leather Jacket, Leather Jacket,
Looks like Leather Jacket
Got the whole packet."

And guess who he was looking at and smiling at this time? Yeah. Which meant, of course, that everyone else was looking at me, too. I smiled to show I was a good sport, which wasn't exactly how I was feeling on the inside. He repeated, this time with a thicker accent:

"Said, oh yeah, Leather Jacket
Got de 'ole packet."

Then he slowed the tune down and belted out,

"Her daddy's rich
And her momma's good-looking."

Which made some people in the audience laugh and clap. I kept smiling and fought off the urge to tell them all that I'd paid for the jacket myself with my babysitting money.

The singer looked back at me with a big smile and a wink while he sang,

"Wish I could get some a
Her home cooking."

Which, yeah, I'll admit was a cheesy rhyme, but

you have to remember that he was making everything up on the spot. And even though I knew it was supposed to be some kind of sexual double entendre, I didn't mind, because it wasn't sleazy. It was fun. I even dug a dollar out of my pocket and tossed it into the guitar case, which inspired one more verse:

"All day long-a,
I strumma this-a tune,
Every once in a blue moon
Someone smile—
Give me a dollar
Without gettin' all hot
Under the collar."

He winked at me and said, "Tank you, Leather Jacket."

As I said, "You're welcome," I suddenly remembered why I was down on Telegraph. I held my camera up and asked, "Um, would you guys mind if I took your picture?"

Still playing his guitar, he smiled and said, "Sure, go ahead."

So I snapped a few of him and his partner. And then I stepped back, so I could get the audience in, too.

× × ×

I forced myself to move down the block. A bunch of the street kids were sitting, playing cards or talking with one another, seemingly oblivious to the people walking by on their way to Telegraph's boutiques and restaurants. I had major butterflies in my stomach as I tried to get up my nerve to approach someone for my story.

One girl was blabbing on a cell phone. If it weren't for the backpack next to her, the rolled-up sleeping bag she sat on, and the sign sitting next to a plastic cup that said

If you
FEAR
CHANGE
leave it here. ☺

I would have thought she was just another EBH girl with her "No way"s and her "Shut up"s. Next to her, two boys sat grooving to a boom box, and a little farther down the block a girl typed furiously on a pretty new-looking laptop.

So maybe the rumor was true. Maybe half the kids who hung out on Telegraph weren't homeless at all, just bored suburban kids who rode BART in for the day and left for the comfort of their own beds at night.

I hate to admit this, but my next thought was maybe the phone, boom box, and laptop were stolen. I tightened my grip on my camera.

× × ×

Riding home from b.t.t. earlier that week, after listening to Dad and Mim argue about whether or not you should give money or food or your home address to street kids, I'd come up with what I thought was a great idea for my Story Hunt project. I would go down to Telegraph and interview some of those kids. I'd try to find out why they were living on the street and what it was like, on a daily basis, to be out there. I'd made a whole list of questions, and I'd envisioned myself kind of like a television reporter, smiling and having pleasant exchanges with my interview subjects. I'd imagined bringing back a touching, beautifully written account of my interviews, along with pictures. All of this would blow Joanna and Nathan away and they would have no choice but to put it on the front page.

But now that I was there, I couldn't bring myself to ask even ask one question. What if no one would talk to me? What if they were mean, like that time I'd gotten yelled at for not giving a dollar when I was asked? And why the hell did I wear the stupid leather jacket? I should have worn my punk makeover outfit. Then I wouldn't stick out so obviously.

I spotted a girl sitting off by herself near the end of the block, dreamily petting a puppy in her lap. I took a few steps closer. She was wearing a hat so I couldn't see her hair, but I was pretty sure she was the green-haired, pale-faced girl who had been part of Jimmy's buffet dinner the other night.

My heart pounded as I walked toward her.

I took a deep breath and said, "Cute puppy."

She looked up. If she recognized me, she didn't show it.

"Thanks." She turned her attention back to the puppy.

"Um . . . hi."

"Hi," she said.

"I'm Kelsey."

"Oh." She left it at that. No "Nice to meet you, my name is . . ."

Okay, different approach.

"What's the puppy's name?"

Her face changed. It wasn't exactly a smile, but

something happened in the vicinity of her mouth. She squeezed the puppy to her chest. "This is Max." She still hadn't looked me in the eye, but at least she was responding.

I squatted down to her and Max's level and reached out. But before putting my hand on him, I asked, "Is it okay?"

"Sure, he loves to be petted, don't you, Max?" She gave him another cuddle-hug before loosening her grip so I could touch the puppy.

"What kind is he?"

She shrugged. "We think he's got some shepherd. See these feet?" She held his brown front paw up for me to inspect. It was big. "Maybe some pit bull. His eyes look like a pit's. Maybe some rotweiller. The nose looks like a rotweiller."

I didn't know a whole lot about dogs, but it sounded like little fuzzy Max might grow up to be a monster.

"People get scared when they hear all that," said the girl, as if she'd read my mind. "But he's sooooooo sweet! Aren't you Maxie boy?" Now she was holding him up in front of her, nose-to-nose. And now she was really smiling.

I took another deep breath. "So, what's your name?"

The smile disappeared. She put Max back in her lap and scratched him behind his floppy ears. For a super-killer dog, he sure was cute. "Are you from Social Services? You doin' your internship for your master's degree and wanna study me?"

"Who, me?" Wow. I'd been mistaken for college-age a few times. But no one had ever accused me of being a graduate student before. "I'm just in high school. I'm a sophomore."

She didn't quite glare, but she looked at me hard. "Oh. 'Cause there was one girl who looked kind of like you snooping around here this summer trying to 'help' me." She put finger quotes around "help."

"Nope. I'm not going to try to help you," I said, which sounded kind of harsh. "I don't know what kind of help *I* could give, anyway."

"Got a dollar? You could help by giving me a dollar. It's not for me. I gotta get Max some Science Diet. He can't eat the cheap stuff. Gives him diarrhea. Right, Maxie?"

"Okay," I said. I had to put the camera down to reach into my pocket. The girl stared at it, and then looked back at me.

"What's that?"

"A camera," I said.

"Yeah, duh. I know it's a camera. What's it for?"

"Well, um . . ." Was there any point in pretending? I held the dollar out. "I'm . . . I was hoping . . . I was going to ask if . . . I could interview you."

She rolled her eyes. "Here we go." She hadn't touched the dollar.

"No. It's not like that—" Not like what? I wondered, even as I said it. "I'm doing a story for my high-school paper. And I thought . . . Well, I wanted to find out about what it was like, to, um—"

"Yeah, yeah," she said, like she'd heard it all before. "And you thought, Hey, I'll go find me a runaway homeless girl for show-and-tell."

"No."

"No? You're not on some how-the-other-half-lives mission?"

"No. No. I was hoping—Well, I *do* want to know how you live. But not like that. Not like that 'other half' stuff. I bet we're more alike than different." She still hadn't taken the dollar, so I dropped my hand down to my lap.

Now she was glaring. First at my leather jacket. Then at my boots, which I'd chosen that morning because I thought they'd make me look more professional, like someone on *20/20* or *Dateline*.

I looked at her shoes. Black Chuck Taylor low tops. Way beyond fashionably well worn. The shoelaces had broken and been retied so now they were too short to make it through all the eyes.

"Okay. I guess that was a dumb thing to say. I really don't know what I'm doing. But, um, do you remember the other night? My family and I walked by you and your friends when you were having dinner on the sidewalk? My grandmother gave you—or, rather, a guy named Jimmy—her fusilli? From b.t.t.? You guys had quite a spread. Bagels, cream cheese—"

"Your grandmother's leftovers. Oh yeah. I remember now, it's all coming back to me. Hard to forget an exquisite meal like that. Did she include the wilted parsley? It's such a nice touch when they include the garnish."

I put my camera back in my messenger bag and started to stand up. "Okay, well, I'm sorry to bother you. Um, do you want this?" I held out the dollar. "I really don't want Max to have diarrhea." I squatted down to scratch him behind the ears one more time. So maybe my brilliant Story Hunt idea wasn't so brilliant. Maybe I would be the prop girl for *Footloose*. Amy said they were desperate.

The girl looked at the dollar in my hand. Then at Max. Then at me. She reached out and took it.

"I can't tell you my real name, because people

might be looking for me. Probably not. They probably won't bother," she scoffed. "But in case they do, I don't want them to find me, so call me Star, okay?"

I squatted down beside her.

"Are we . . . Are you . . . Is this an interview?"

"Hope you have some better questions than that, Newsgirl."

19

Write What You Know; You Know Some Things

I went home with three pages of notes, thirty minutes of tape, and a bunch of pictures.

It's not like Star totally opened up and told me her life story or anything. I got the feeling that she was leaving a lot out. But she did tell me some about why she left home in the first place, and why she didn't want to stay in the foster home she got sent to, and why she doesn't go to one of the teen shelters in San Francisco.

"One," she said, holding out her thumb, "they won't let me have Max. Two"—she released her index finger—"Clay and I would have to sleep separately. Three"—her middle finger joined the others—"I *can't* sleep if I don't have my boys with me. Max on one side and Clay on the other. We're a family. I mean, it's not like we're going to have sex in a room we have to share with a bunch of other people. That is totally gross. Believe me, I've seen it."

Clay is Star's boyfriend. He showed up toward the end of my interview with Star. He'd been at a Laundromat, washing their clothes, which I thought was pretty amazing of him. Star told me that normally they did laundry together every Saturday (that was another surprising thing—their life had a lot more structure than I would have guessed), but she was having really bad cramps and Clay had insisted on going himself.

"He takes good care of me," she said. "Better than anyone else ever has."

I thought about how C.J. always used to get a little pale whenever I'd talked about anything remotely menstrual.

× × ×

It took some convincing, because Star has a really proud streak, but when our interview was over, she let me buy her a piece of pizza at Fat Slice. Clay came, too.

He had matching green hair and looked even younger than Star. Maybe it was just because he was so skinny, but I would have guessed he was fifteen, tops.

They were an adorable couple. Called each other "honey" and touched a lot, but not in that annoying, show-offy way some couples do just so you know things are hot between them. With Star and Clay it seemed more real, like they truly cared about each other.

I took a bunch of pictures while we were at Fat Slice—which was a long time, because Star ate three pieces and Clay two.

"Guess you're feeling better," Clay said when she started in on the third.

Star shrugged. "Yeah. I'm starved."

× × ×

My favorite picture of them was a close-up. Clay's head was leaning in, just slightly, toward Star's, like he was going to kiss her or tell her a secret. The corners of his mouth were turned up in a little smile. She was leaning in to him, too, and the tough-girl expression was totally gone from her face. Their eyes were locked on each other's and I can't even explain it, but you could see they were truly in love, that it wasn't just a sex thing.

She looked even younger on film. Vulnerable. I guess the tough way she talks makes her seem older in person. Looking at him looking at her, I could totally understand why she'd trade the warmth of a shelter bed for the comfort of Clay by her side.

× × ×

By Sunday night, I must've listened to the tape six times—all the way through. I'd read over my notes and stared at the pictures for hours, and I still had no idea how to begin.

I wrote ten versions of an opening sentence, and each time I'd try to move on, I'd hear the voices of the editors echoing in my brain.

Joanna: "You need a hook, something to pull the reader in."

Nathan: "Save a power punch for the end; leave people thinking."

As if that wasn't confusing enough, I kept hearing Star's voice taunting me, "Hey, I'll go find me a runaway homeless girl for show-and-tell."

Ever since sitting with her for the interview, and then with her and Clay after that, I hadn't been able to get her out of my head. When I sat down for dinner with my family, I wondered where Star was, and what she was having for dinner. Or if she was even having dinner.

After talking with her that afternoon, I knew I wasn't going to be able to just walk by those kids again. I wanted to write her story in a way that would get people to feel how I felt talking to her. I wanted to write something that would get people like me—and maybe even people like my dad, who assumed the worst about the kids on Telegraph—to look a little harder next time they walked by.

But I had no idea how to get that all down on paper.

I sent a desperate e-mail to Mr. Rundle, warning him that I'd be in for an early-morning visit. He'd help me figure out where to start.

He hadn't answered by the time I went to bed, or by the time I got up the next morning, but I set out for the early bus, anyway.

× × ×

East Bay High doesn't look so bad on a Monday morning at 6:15. It's incredibly quiet, and cleaner than usual. Despite the principal's pleas and the efforts of the Campus Conservation Club, whose posters scolded us as we walked down the hall

A Cleaner Environment Begins with You

(Yeah, YOU!)

Don't Trash (Y)Our School

the place was usually pretty litter-strewn, especially after lunch.

Mr. Rundle's trailer was dark, but there was light coming from *The Bee* office. I peeked through the smudged window to see the unmistakable back of Nathan's curly head. He was sitting at a computer, his iPod's earphones in, and from the look of his shoulders, he was rocking out.

He must have had the volume way up, because no matter how hard I banged on the door, he never turned around. He was typing and clicking, typing and clicking, working in what looked like five different windows. At one point, he turned on a second computer, and started rolling between the two. I was about to give up trying to get his attention when I noticed a small window above one of the two computers he was using. I walked around the trailer, but it was too high for me to reach on my own. But by climbing the railing that surrounded the trailer, I could see in perfectly.

Nathan had the most intense concentration I'd ever seen. I banged and waved and banged and waved and almost fell a couple times before finally, *finally* catching his eye.

"Can you let me in?" I shouted into the glass.

"What?"

I pointed to the door behind him. He nodded, then used his legs to push himself toward it in his wheeled chair. I climbed down and ran around.

"Hey, cub. What up?" he said, pushing the door open for me. He still hadn't gotten out of his chair. One earphone was dangling off his shoulders and I could hear Bob Marley asking if I could *be loved, and be lo-oved.*

"Um, well, I was hoping to see Mr. Rundle. Do you know when he usually gets in?"

"Rundle-man went away for the weekend," said Nathan, as he rolled himself back to the computers where he'd been working. "Says he'll be here in time for his first class."

"Oh."

"You have a paper or something?" he said into his shoulder as he was typing and clicking.

"Sort of."

"Oh yeah? What on? You're a sophomore, right? Let me see if I remember. Sophomore year, you're reading *Huck Finn*?" He was studying his monitor.

I shook my head. He looked back at me.

"*For Whom the Bell Tolls*?"

I shook my head again. "Well, we are reading those this year, but we don't have papers due yet. I was actually hoping Mr. Rundle might help me figure out what to do with my Story Hunt piece."

"Oh yeah? Cool. What'd you come up with?"

"Well, it's not really done yet. I just did an interview, but I have no idea what to do next. You know, how to put it into a story. Yesterday, I spent the whole day going over and over my material."

"That sounds good. So you really know it then?"

"I guess." I had pretty much memorized everything Star had said.

"Okay," said Nathan, patting the desk next to him. "So pull up a chair and write."

"Right now? Here?"

"Yup. What you need is a deadline, and the clatter of the newsroom. That's how most newspaper writing is done. I did an internship at the *Chronicle* last year. You'd be amazed at how loud it gets, and people still crank it out for their deadlines."

"But I don't know where to start."

"Look, you've had Mr. Rundle, right?"

I nodded.

"And what's the first Rundle-ism?"

Together, Nathan and I said, "Write what you know; you know some things."

"What's your topic?"

"Well . . . that's part of the problem. I'm not really sure."

"I thought you said you did interviews. You don't know what you talked about?" At that moment, I felt like I really could read minds. I'm sure that some version of *Could this girl possibly be as dumb as that?* passed through Nathan's brain.

"One interview. Of one girl. One of the kids who hangs out down on Telegraph."

"Cool," said Nathan, nodding. "We did a story on street kids a couple of years ago."

"Oh, I didn't know." Of course they had. Why did I think I was doing something new?

"But that's okay. It's an ongoing issue. I'm sure you'll bring a fresh approach. And besides, the Story Hunt's supposed to be about learning, right? So sit down here and . . . let's see. . . ." He looked at his watch. "Give me an article in an hour. Five hundred words or so."

× × ×

If someone had asked me to describe what I thought were the ideal circumstances for writing my first newspaper article, I would never have said, "Sitting next to the really cute, really smart co-editor in chief while he's jamming away to Bob Marley and typing and clicking and occasionally singing a little too loudly at the next computer."

But surprisingly, these circumstances actually did get me to crank something out. Because what the hell else was I going to do at 6:30 A.M. sitting next to the really cute, really smart co-editor in chief who's jamming away to Bob Marley and typing and clicking and occasionally singing a little too loudly at the next computer?

I pulled out my notes and my transcript of the interview, and I just dove in. I typed pretty much nonstop, going back over sentences now and then to smooth them out.

And so within a mere thirty-seven minutes, I had 504 words.

CALL HER STAR
by Kelsey Wilcox
504 words

Have you ever wondered what happens to that doughy hunk of Fat Slice crust that you toss, absentmindedly, in the trash on your way to check out the latest fall (or spring or summer or winter) fashions at ShoeTique on Telegraph? Did you ever stop to ask yourself whether the person whose legs you step over on your way to buy those chunky-heeled black boots you've drooled over for weeks and finally talked your mom into forking over the cash for has a name?

Maybe, like this reporter, you wondered how someone could go out in public in shoes that were falling apart like hers, not thinking that perhaps this was her only pair, and that she did not have the luxury of changing shoes with the seasons or even once in a day because the only clothes she had were what she was wearing, and what she could carry in her backpack. Or that maybe "out in public" was where she was pretty much living her life?

Well, her name is Star, or at least that's what she goes by out here on the street.

"I'm not telling you my real name, 'cause people might come looking for me and I don't want to be found right now."

Star is sixteen. She's originally from Oregon. She came to Berkeley with her boyfriend, Clay, because "the weather's okay if you have to sleep outside, and you can get free breakfasts and there are always kids here on Telegraph just hanging out, and it's way better than where I came from."

When asked to explain what she means about where she comes from, Star shrugs. "Oh, you know, the usual runaway story. Dead mother, alcoholic, unemployed father. Blah blah blah."

When asked whether she ever tried to get help, she shrugs. "Yeah. They put me in a foster home, but that was a joke. My foster so-called brother came in my room in the middle of the night, thinking we were going to get to know each other better. I climbed right out the window and never looked back."

I asked Star to describe some of the practical problems of life on the street. On the question of how she stores and cares for her clothes, she says, "Everything I own, I carry with me. Me and Clay do laundry once a week." On personal grooming: "The city lets us shower over at the locker room of the public pool. Make sure you tell them I'm clean. I take a shower every other day."

Star also wants people to know that she is a law-abiding citizen. "I always pick up after my dog," she says, pulling a handful of plastic grocery bags out of her back pocket. "Make sure you tell people that we pick up after our dog! I see the way people look at me when they walk by, like I'm dirty, like I'm garbage littering their streets."

Her name is Star. She doesn't litter.

And you know what? She isn't litter, either!

I spell-checked it and read it over with twelve minutes to spare.

From the look on his face and the way he kept starting and stopping, I gathered Nathan was IMing someone. Miss Italy maybe?

I clicked PRINT, and as the printer across the room started to hum, the trailer door opened, and in walked Joanna. Nathan was in his own little Bob Marley world, smiling at his monitor and typing furiously.

"What's this?" she said, looking at Nathan's back, then at me.

"Hi, Joanna," I said, blushing up to my ears. "I . . . um. Nathan was just helping me—" I reached out to tap him on the shoulder. "Nathan?"

He pulled his earphones out again. I could hear *I don't want to wait in vain for your love* perfectly clear. "Done? That was fast."

"Yeah . . . um." I looked to Joanna

"Hi, Nathan," said Joanna. She had a hand on her hip. She was doing something weird with her lips that twisted up her whole face.

Nathan looked at her. "Oh, hey." He glanced back at his monitor and reached out and flipped a switch. The screen went dark. "'Sup, Jo?"

"Holding a little early-morning tutoring session?" She walked over behind us, looked at his dark monitor, then at mine. Then at me.

"No," he said, sounding more than a little defensive. "Well, I was helping Kelsey here with her Story Hunt project—unofficially. We just both happened to be here early."

"IwaslookingforMr.Rundle," I said to Joanna. It was a totally normal thing to do and to say, but it came out really fast, and unfortunately loud, like I was hiding something.

This was totally weird. Nathan and Joanna reminded me of my parents during the pre-Stan days when they were so hostile to each other that I hated being with both of them in the same room.

"Yeah, so Kelsey here went down to Telegraph over the weekend and did some interviews."

"One interview. And I took some pictures," I said, nodding toward the folder where I'd put the printouts.

"Oh? Huh." She walked over to the printer and picked up my story. My heart, which I'd thought was already pounding as much as it could pound, started working even harder. "We did a series on those kids a couple years ago. Didn't Ellen get a prize for that? A gold medal from the state?" She started reading my piece.

Nathan shrugged. He'd rolled over to the file folder, which I'd left open next to me. "Well, you know, three-quarters of our readership has turned over since then. So it'll be—" He stopped talking as he picked up the pictures of Star sitting on the sidewalk with Max, and later with Clay at Fat Slice. "Wow." He looked at me. "You took these?"

"Yup." I looked back at Joanna, who had taken out a red pen and started circling and underlining and scribbling in the margins of my story.

"They're nice. You really caught something here."

"Thanks."

He put those pictures down and picked up the one with the musician guys. "I see you met Sean and Vonn," he said.

"Who?"

Joanna still had her nose in—and her red pen on—my story.

Nathan held up the picture. "Sean and Vonn. They go to Scholastic. Sean tells me they make a killing down there."

"They're not homeless or runaways or whatever?"

"Hardly." Nathan shook his head and smiled. "Sean's parents are both doctors. And Vonn's family owns a whole chain of restaurants."

"But they sing all these songs about life on the street, like it's where they live."

"I know. Pretty audacious, huh?"

"Yeah."

"At first it was an experiment—a research project. Kind of like what you were doing. They wanted to see what kind of money street musicians make. Guess they do pretty well."

"I think it's creepy," said Joanna, as she walked over to join us. I had to agree. "We should out them."

Nathan laughed. "Right."

"I'm serious. It's fraud. We should publish these pictures and go over to Scholastic and get some of them in their blue blazers."

"Oh, come on, lighten up. If people get sucked in, that's their problem."

I thought about how the real street kids—like Star and Clay—had to rely on what they could scrounge together with odd jobs and begging. And how much less money was in their cups and jars than in Sean and Vonn's guitar case. I thought Joanna had a point.

Joanna didn't bother answering Nathan. She just shot him a look, and the subject was dropped. She turned to me and held out my story. It was oozing red ink. "So, cub. It's a little chatty."

"Chatty?"

"Yeah, chatty," said Joanna. "All that 'Did you

ever wonder?' and the stuff about shoes and shopping and ShoeTique."

"Hold up, hold up. Let me see that." Nathan got up out of his chair and grabbed my story out of her hands.

"Hey!"

"Hey what? I need to know what you're talking about."

Joanna turned her back to Nathan. "Anyway, as I was saying, Kelsey, your personal shopping habits are not supposed to be a part of the story. That's the first commandment of reporting. You've got to be an objective eye. You're supposed to present your subjects directly to the reader. You have to leave yourself out."

I looked over at Nathan, who was looking at Joanna and shaking his head.

She glared at him, arms folded in front of her chest.

"Nathan? Did you want to say something?"

"Yeah. I want to say, 'Can you give me a minute to read this before you start making executive decisions here?' "

She threw her hands up. "Be my guest."

Okay. So then I had to sit there, staring at my computer screen, while Nathan read through the piece.

It took two minutes and fourteen seconds. First he sort of smiled. Then he sort of laughed. Then he took out a pen and circled something, and made a note in the margin. Finally he looked up.

"You know, I actually think it works. The contrast between the mindless shopper and the street kids. Her thoughts provide a frame of reference, a link between our world and the world of the kids on the street. Maybe we could run it as an opinion piece sometime. With these pictures . . ." He pulled my photos out of a folder and handed the one of Star and Clay locked in that lovey look to Joanna. "It could make a nice spread."

She scowled as she held the picture in front of her. "We don't usually put cubs on the Op-Ed page. I didn't get my first Op-Ed piece until the end of my sophomore year. And I started as a freshman." She looked over at me as she said that.

Nathan shrugged. "Yeah, well . . ."

"Well what?" she said, or rather shouted. She took a step toward him, which was also a step toward me, which meant that I could see how her eyes were tearing up.

"It's not about you, Jo. It's about *The Bee*."

The door to *The Bee* trailer slammed once again

and all three of us turned to find Mr. Rundle standing in the doorway.

"Editorial meeting?"

"Not exactly," said Nathan, looking down at the floor.

"I just came in to get caught up with some stuff and I find Nathan here, making decisions on his own, promising people that their stories are going to run before I've even been consulted." Those tears I'd seen in Joanna's eyes had dried up, along with any sympathy I might have been starting to feel for her.

"I wasn't—you're the one making decisions without consulting me."

"Whoa. Stop. Right there." Mr. Rundle held his hand out in front of him. "You two. In my office. Kelsey, I'll see you in class later, okay? I've got to play referee here." He nodded his head toward Joanna and Nathan, who were both looking at the floor.

I packed up my stuff while the two of them shuffled silently into Mr. Rundle's room.

20

Inexperience Can Be an Asset

"Don't say you weren't warned," Amy said, after I recounted the morning's events in *The Bee* office for her. It was lunchtime, and we were sitting on the steps in front of school. "I can't believe you want to have anything to do with either of them." She took two foil-wrapped burritos out of the paper bag in front of her. "Why don't they put stickers on these things? How are we supposed to know whose is whose?"

She picked up one and sniffed. "Oh." She held it out for me. "This is definitely the chicken."

"Yeah, well, the thing is," I said, unwrapping my burrito, "I think I really like this reporting stuff. I have a lot to learn, but, you know, I was totally into writing that story. Are you sure this is chicken?" I held it out to look inside. "I only see beans and rice."

Amy stopped as she was about to take a bite and held the other burrito out in front of her. She pinched a little hole in the tortilla and peeked in. "Oh, thank God you stopped me." We switched and continued.

"When I was talking to Star and Clay this weekend, I wasn't thinking about what I looked like, or who saw me, or what anyone thought of me. I was just trying to understand how these kids came to be living the life they're living. I know this might sound nuts, but I kind of feel like I was meant to do this."

Amy nodded while she chewed and swallowed. "That's how I feel about drama. Like I can't not do it."

"Yeah. Like that. So I guess I'll just have to figure out how to deal with the ex-power couple. Or the power ex-couple, or whatever they are."

"Speaking of which . . ." Amy's eyes widened at something behind me. I turned to look over my shoulder and barely had a chance to take a breath before Nathan was sitting next to me.

"Hey," he said to me, and then to Amy, "Aren't you Ruth's sister?"

Amy nodded.

"How's she doing? She's at UCLA, right?"

"Great. She's doing great."

"Tell her Nathan says hey for me, okay?"

Then turning back to me, he said, "Listen, I'm

sorry about this morning. Joanna and I . . . Well, we're still trying to figure stuff out. Like how this co-editor thing's going to work and . . . well, it's complicated. But we're determined."

Amy and I looked at each other. *Stuff like how her boyfriend of three years dumped her by e-mail*?

"And so, after Mr. Rundle did his little intervention thing, the three of us talked over your story, and we all agreed that it's a definite contender for publication. You didn't exactly conform to standard news style, but the piece has a style of its own. We're going to hold on to it and see what the rest of the cubs come up with before we make any decisions." Nathan waved to someone behind me.

I turned around and there was Joanna, smiling. Or, well, contorting her face into a not-bad imitation of a smile. She was heading for us.

I glanced over at Amy, who looked like she couldn't wait to see what happened next.

Joanna sat down on my other side. I saw her glance over to the minuscule space between Nathan's leg and mine. For a second, the pseudo-smile disappeared and her face twisted up. But before I knew it, she was back in my face, smiling aggressively.

"So, first of all, I'm sorry you had to witness that

unpleasantness this morning." She looked at Nathan. He shrugged.

Amy moved her eyes side to side between Joanna and Nathan and then raised her eyebrows. I had to look away from her to keep from cracking up, but Nathan and Joanna didn't notice. They were too busy staring each other down.

"Second of all," said Joanna, turning to me, "good job. That piece you wrote will definitely be a contender for publication."

She reached out and squeezed my arm. I tried not to flinch.

"Thanks." I guess. "I thought you thought it sucked."

"Oh come on, 'sucked' is way too strong. It's true I had some issues with the style, but Nathan and Mr. Rundle got me to see how your writing brings a fresh perspective to the runaway situation."

"They did?"

"Yeah. And they were right: Sometimes inexperience *can* be an asset."

"Oh."

"You aren't limited by the usual journalistic protocols."

"Hmm."

"Not knowing what you're doing actually turned out to be a good thing here."

"It did?"

"Yeah. Nathan was right. The persona you created—" She turned to Nathan. "How did you put it, Nate? 'The spoiled rich girl goes slumming'?"

Nathan stopped smiling and shook his head. "I didn't say 'spoiled,' Jo, I said—"

"Mindless," I said. "You said 'mindless shopper.' "

"Yeah, I said 'mindless shopper,' " he said to Joanna. Then, turning to me, like it was dawning on him for the first time that this could be an insult, he said, "And I meant that I thought you had succeeded in using the point of view of a person who goes down to Telegraph Avenue for the boutiques, not that *you* were a mindless shopper. It's a device. And you used it well."

Okay. But this so-called device just happened to closely resemble me. Is this how Nathan saw me? As a mindless, a.k.a. spoiled, rich girl?

"Well, whatever you did," said Joanna, "there's a real spark there. I think you're going to be good at this, Kelsey."

"Really?"

"Yes. I mean you already are good, you just need

to learn some more of the basics. And I'm going to personally help you do that."

"You are?"

"Yeah. I'm going to have you work on a couple of stories with me, so I can help you learn the basics. You know, information-gathering, standard news style, stuff like that. Once you have those down, there'll be no stopping you."

"Okay." I guess.

Joanna leaned out over me to talk to Nathan. "I'm thinking of bringing her in on that story I told you about."

"Which story?"

"The budget thing."

"The budget thing . . . the budget thing."

"The story about the ratio of administrative to instructional spending?"

"Oh, right." Nathan nodded and stood up. "Listen, you guys, I have to get to physics." He turned to me. "You know, a lot of people totally flake on these assignments. Rundle was right. You've definitely got potential."

"Exactly," said Joanna. "Which is why I want her to be the one who helps me with the archival research for this piece."

"Uh-huh." Nathan put a foot up on a step, but before he could move, Joanna grabbed his arm. He looked at her hand on his wrist. "Um, I've got a bus to catch?"

"Oh, that's right. I forgot." She didn't let go. "You take *college* physics."

"Yeah? What's your point?"

"Nothing. No point, Nathan."

He pulled his arm away and headed down the steps.

"Go on with your busy life."

21

In the Closet ~~On the Street~~ with Newsgirl

"This might *seem* dull and pointless," Joanna said, "but we absolutely must have these numbers to have a story. It's a crucial piece of the puzzle."

Joanna and I were in a storage closet in the basement of the Board of Education building, a few blocks from school. She'd walked me there during seventh period to show me how to find the numbers for a story on educational spending trends.

"If we can prove what I think we can prove, this'll be huge. And if we can scoop a couple more stories, they'll have to give us a gold medal this year."

It had been four years since *The Bee* won a Gold Medal for Excellence in High School Journalism. It was kind of like an honor roll for student newspapers. Only five out of hundreds of schools got golds.

There'd been bronzes and silvers and honorable mentions, but no golds for EBH in a while. Joanna was determined to get the gold before she left for college.

"If we get a gold while I'm editor in chief, I'll feel like I've done my job. Like I've lived up to *The Bee* tradition."

She squatted down to the bottom shelf and grabbed a binder marked 1951–1952 and then sat back on the floor, patting the space beside her for me to sit, too. The binder contained page after page of yellowed paper, each with seemingly endless columns of numbers. Big numbers.

"Okay. We're tracing five decades of spending. The last two are online, so don't worry about those. I'll get them myself." She needed me to look up the other thirty years' worth and fill them in on the spreadsheet she'd created and loaded onto my laptop. Once we had the numbers, Joanna was going to run them through a program that would chart changes in the proportion of administrative to instructional spending.

"We go to press Monday and we won't have access over the weekend. So I need these by Friday. Do you think you can do it?"

It didn't seem that complicated. Granted, standing in a dusty, windowless closet wasn't going to be as much fun as roaming the streets, taking pictures and doing interviews. But I figured if I followed Joanna's lead, I'd be getting more of those assignments eventually.

"Sure."

Tuesday, I worked all of seventh period plus an extra hour, and I only managed to get through the first three years' records.

By Wednesday, I felt like I was going cross-eyed. It seemed that every year, the people who kept these records had reinvented their system. Finding the right numbers and then getting them in the right place on the spreadsheet was taking way longer than Joanna seemed to think it should.

"Come on, cub, I'm counting on you," she said after I showed her my progress on Wednesday afternoon. I'd stayed till five, when the Board of Ed closed, and still I'd only gotten up to 1964–1965.

Thursday night, by special arrangement with Coleman the security guard, I stayed until seven o'clock, the latest Mim and Mom would agree to.

I got to the seventies by Friday. That's when the notebooks turned into these big, heavy piles of computer printouts—miles and miles of blue and white paper folded accordion-style and bound and clipped in cardboard covers. By four o'clock, I still had five more years to go.

I called *The Bee* office. Maybe if someone could come over and read the numbers to me, I could finish in time for Joanna to run the numbers over the weekend.

No one answered, so I left a message, desperately trying not to sound desperate. "Hi. This is Kelsey and I was just wondering if there was anyone around who might help me finish up with these numbers? I'm very close to finishing, but Coleman the security guard says I have to be out of here by seven because some other guy is going to finish up his shift for him because he has As tickets, and it's the playoffs. . . ."

I pictured my voice talking to the darkened, empty trailer. Even Mr. Rundle, who seemed to spend all his time at school, wouldn't be there this late on a Friday. I started to feel sorry for myself, which was a mistake, because then my voice got a little trembly. "And well, if there's anyone around who can help me, I'm in the basement of the Board of Ed. Just ask Coleman to show you the way."

I took a deep breath, pulled 1973–1974 from the

shelf, sank down next to my laptop, and started flipping through the stiffened pages. I was not going to give up. I was not going to give Joanna reason to doubt me, and I was not going to be the reason *The Bee* didn't get a gold medal this year.

It might have been my sighing, or it might have been the crackling of the computer printouts that hadn't been looked at in thirty years. But for some reason, I didn't hear any footsteps coming down the hall, or the closet door swing open, and so when Nathan said, "Hey," I screamed.

"Whoa. Whoa. Sorry. I didn't mean to scare you." He walked over to where I was slumped against the wall, leaned down, and squeezed my shoulder. "I heard your message."

My heart was pounding, and it wasn't showing any signs of slowing down. Not only had I just been startled completely out of my wits, I was now sitting in a storage closet with Nathan Wexler. And Nathan Wexler had just touched me. Apparently, the little crush I was doing my best to ignore was doing its best to ignore the list of very good reasons to avoid involvement with Nathan Wexler, at the top of which was:

a.) The fact that getting together with a new guy

probably wasn't going to help undo whatever damage C.J. had done to my reputation.

And if that didn't do it, there were all of these reasons:

b.) The matter of the electronic breakup. Even if the relationship was over, and even if your ex-girlfriend is Joanna Breslin, what kind of person ends a three-year relationship by e-mail—from Europe?

c.) The matter of the Italian contessa. (Granted, no one could say for sure that she existed, but Nathan did seem to spend a lot of time IMing someone. Usually when a guy's IMing like that, there's a girl out there somewhere, squirming for every chime.)

d.) The wrath of Joanna—which should have been reason enough.

But judging by my body's response to being in close proximity to Nathan's body, none of these reasons was convincing.

I pictured the calm lady on this yoga DVD Mim and I sometimes do together. *Breathe in through your nose. Breathe to the very bottom of your lungs. Now hold, and slowwwwwly let it out through your mouth.*

Well that backfired. By the time I let out the last

bit of air, I'd given myself a wicked case of hiccups.

Nathan pulled a water bottle out of his backpack. "Go ahead. It's brand-new. Untouched by human lips."

Something about Nathan's using the words "lips" and "touch" in the same sentence sent my blushing level back up to maximum. I managed to take a few big slugs of water. If Nathan noticed that some of it drooled out of the side of my mouth, he kindly ignored it.

But the water did nothing for the hiccups.

Nathan said, "I've had a lot of success with the tie-your-shoes while swallowing upside-down method." We both looked down at my feet. I was wearing my new fall boots. No laces.

Nathan slid his foot up alongside mine. "Be my guest." He wore black suede Vans—exactly the same shoes C.J. always wore. That made my stomach do a little flip. Not that it meant anything. Probably half the guys in our school owned a pair of black suede Vans. "Okay," he said, reaching out for the bottle and lifting it toward my mouth. "When you're ready, take a big gulp of water, bend at the waist, and swallow slowly while tying the shoes."

There's something weirdly intimate about tying

another person's shoes. I'd never done it for anyone except Josh, the kids I babysat for, and Mim, when her back was bothering her. Even though it was just his feet, this was the closest I'd been to Nathan's body. It was the closest I'd been to any male body since C.J.

When I stood back up, the hiccups were gone, but the stubborn attraction to Nathan wasn't.

I decided the best strategy was to concentrate on the task at hand. It took a few minutes for me to explain how the spreadsheet was organized and how to enter the numbers, but eventually Nathan and I settled into a routine. I stood in front of the shelves, flipping through the printouts and reading the numbers to him while he sat on the floor entering them on the computer.

After we got through the first year, Nathan said, "Tell me why we're doing this again?"

"It's for that budget study."

"Right. The budget study. And we're studying the budget because . . . ?"

"Didn't you and Joanna talk about this?"

He shrugged. "Kind of. She talked. I pretended to listen."

"Oh. It's because she thinks she can show that while overall education spending has gone up, the ratio of administrative to instructional . . ."

Nathan closed his eyes, dropped his head to the side and let out a loud, fake snore. Then another. And another.

"Hey." I stretched my leg out and nudged his foot, laughing.

He opened his eyes and shook his head. "Wha'? Wha'?"

"The ratio of administrative spending to . . ."

He started to close his eyelids again. I laughed and talked louder, going along with the game.

". . . to instructional spending has increased dramatically."

He dropped his head again and fell backward, as if he'd passed out. Something about the way he hit the metal shelf behind him caused it to come loose from one of its brackets. Several years' worth of bound computer printouts went tumbling to the floor and onto the shelf below, which caused that shelf to come loose from both brackets. Those printouts landed on the floor with a loud thump and the shelf came clattering after. Luckily, the metal bracket that bounced off Nathan's thigh didn't do any damage.

"Oh shit," Nathan whispered after the clattering finally stopped. We both looked at the half-open door leading to the hallway and Coleman-the-security-guard's desk. We sat still for a while, until it seemed safe to assume no one had heard.

It took us a while to get the shelves back together and return the printouts to their proper shelves. Some of the pages had gotten bent, and a few of the perforated edges had torn, but I was pretty sure no one but us had looked at these records since they were put here twenty years before, so I wasn't worried.

When we were almost through cleaning up our mess, I said, "I take it you think this is a stupid idea for an article? Do you see eighty-eighty-one anywhere?"

"Stupid? I wouldn't go that far." Nathan pulled 1980–81 across the floor and bent down to pick it up. "These things must weigh ten pounds apiece. But it's not like people are going to be lining up waiting to get their hands on the results of *The Bee*'s school board budget study." He stood up next to me, close enough so that the sides of our arms were touching.

Maybe Nathan had one of those social disorders Mim told me about that makes you insensitive to the personal space needs of others.

"But Joanna—" Now I could feel his hip bone against mine. It was getting hard to think.

"Joanna is out-of-her-mind stressed. She's convinced herself that if she doesn't get *The Bee* a gold medal this year, she'll never get into Yale. And if she doesn't get into Yale, her life will be over. She's got a bunch of different articles going, hoping one of them will be the story that clinches the gold and her early acceptance."

"Really? But this is going to be next week's lead story, right?"

"Is that what she said? Maybe." He shrugged and stepped to the side, creating space between us. The places where his arms and hips had been pressing against mine felt cold. "We never know for sure until the night we go to print. Depends on what else we have. Whether any big stories come in. It could be the lead if it's a relatively slow news week."

"Oh." I was trying to remember what Joanna's exact words were, and why I had the impression I was working on a front-page story, when my cell rang.

"You poor thing." It was Joanna. "I'll be right over."

"Oh. Um. That's okay. We're just finishing up."

"We?"

I snuck a look at Nathan, he was focused on the spreadsheet. "Yeah." I tried to sound as matter-of-fact as I could, which just made me sound like I was trying to sound matter-of-fact. "Nathan helped me."

Nathan looked up and mouthed, "Is that Joanna?"

I nodded.

"Nathan helped you." The *poor thing* tone disappeared.

"Yeah, I guess he checked the messages and—"

"He told me he was going to be in physics lab all afternoon."

"Oh. Um . . ." I looked to Nathan.

"Did he mention his physics lab to you?" Joanna asked.

This was truly icky. "To tell you the truth . . ." *To tell you the truth*? I never said, *To tell you the truth.* "We've just been cranking on these numbers." That wasn't exactly the truth. "And you'll be happy to know we just have two more years and you'll be able to crunch them." But that was the truth. We were almost done.

"Oh."

"So I'll e-mail the spreadsheet to you as soon as I get home?"

"Okay." Almost the second "Call Ended" appeared on my screen, Nathan's cell rang.

"Wow, her speed dial is speedy." He slipped his phone out of his pocket, flipped it open, and without bothering to read the caller ID, said, "Hey."

Joanna was so loud, Nathan had to hold the phone away from his ear. I couldn't hear the words, but from the sound of her voice, she was pissed. After she'd gone on for a while, Nathan said, "Um, Jo?" But she didn't stop. She got even louder. He moved the phone farther away from his ear, and that's when I was pretty sure I heard "C.J. Logan." It could have been "our new slogan," but I was pretty sure, by the way Nathan's eyes snuck a quick look at me and pulled the phone back into his ear that Joanna was talking about C.J. and not some new advertising campaign strategy.

Rather than stand there and watch while Nathan took in the misinformation about me and my liar of an ex-boyfriend, I started to flip through the print-out, doing my best to look like I was concentrating on the numbers and not on the conversation that was occurring three feet away from me.

"What's that got to do with anything, Jo?"

Nathan got quiet. Joanna didn't. I couldn't hear her words, but her voice carried over to my side of the closet just fine.

He said, "Jo? Joanna? No. That's not what's going on."

He put the palm of his non-phone-holding hand to his forehead and rubbed while she went on.

"I'm going to hang up now, okay?"

. . .

"Actually, I didn't mean it as a question."

. . .

"No. No. No. You're wrong. I was on my way but then I decided to stop by the office to check my e-mail, and that's when I got her message."

I snuck a look over my shoulder and saw Nathan standing there, holding the phone away from his ear with one hand while rubbing his forehead with the other. He glanced over at me and then turned so his back was toward me. He was trying to speak softly, but the space we were standing in was so small, there was no way I could not hear him.

"Jo, my e-mail isn't any of your business anymore." He took a step toward the door. "Not that it was before, but now . . ."

. . .

"Oh, come on, like you don't use those machines for personal stuff? Just—Jo—Can't we please just act professional, like we agreed?" He took another step toward the door.

. . .

"You're the one who dreamed up this ridiculous assignment—the Board of Education budget? What is *that* about?" With that, he stepped out the door and into the empty hallway, pulling the closet door behind him. The last words I heard were "So now you're trying to—" And then all I could hear was his voice, echoing in the hall.

I sat there staring at the 1985 Board of Education budget, forcing myself to enter the numbers in my laptop, one digit at a time, trying not to try to hear what Nathan was saying out in the hall. After a few more exchanges, the door swung back open and Nathan came sighing in.

"So . . . Sorry about that. Joanna's . . . She's just . . ."

"Upset."

"Yeah, I guess you could say. It's hard. We were together for a long time . . . and it's . . ."

"Complicated."

"Yeah." He ran his fingers through his hair, squeezed his curls, and let go, leaving a little clump sticking out on the side. "So, um. Why don't we wrap this up and you and Joanna can take it from here. I've got to get back to Cal to finish up that lab, anyway."

For the whole rest of the time we were there, Nathan kept his distance. He slid the laptop down the shelf until he was about five feet away from me. He didn't look up once as I read the final numbers to him, and when the last number was entered, he practically ran out of the storage closet.

22

Toxic Shock

"Look at this." Monday morning, I plopped the new *Bee* down in front of Amy, who was typing away madly on her laptop at our booth at the Hut. IMing Mr. Seattle, no doubt.

"Just a—" Her eyes didn't leave the screen as she tapped a few more keys, a huge smile on her face. Finally she looked up. "What?"

"That," I said, pointing to the teeny tiny italicized words at the bottom of the very last column on the back page. It was at the end of Joanna's story on administrative spending in the Board of Education budget, which was underneath Joanna's story of the debate team's triumph at the regional championship.

Amy squinted. "'Kelsey Wilcox contributed to this article,'" she read aloud. "That's good, isn't it?"

"'Kelsey Wilcox contributed to this article?' *That's* my thanks for five days in the dusty dungeon? Kelsey Wilcox contributed to this puny little boring nobody's-going-to-read article on the back page? It's a stupid article, I'll admit. But I did all the research."

"Really?" Amy's eyes were back on her computer screen. "Bummer."

"That's not the worst of it, though. Check out the front page."

She flipped the paper over. That got her attention. "What the—?"

Soaring above the fold with a crowd of open-mouthed admirers behind him was C.J. Logan. The headline said, TOXIC PUDDLE FORCES SKATEPARK CLOSURE. Byline? Who else? Joanna Breslin. I sat down next to Amy while she read the article.

> *The city of Berkeley ordered CitySkate Park closed yesterday, when groundwater polluted with a carcinogenic chemical seeped into the bowls of the skatepark. The water contained hexavalent chromium, the cancer-causing agent made famous in the movie "Erin Brockovich." The chemical had been used in a nearby building that once housed a chrome-plating factory.*

"It's important to note that we're talking about groundwater, not drinking water, which was the case in that movie," says Evan Henry, a spokesperson for the California Office of Environmental Health Hazard Assessment. "But this stuff can be dangerous if it becomes airborne," he added.

Hexavalent chromium can cause lung cancer and severe birth defects.

(see Skatepark, p. 2, column a)

"This stuff sounds scary," said Amy, turning to page two, where, above the rest of the story, there were two more pictures, one of C.J. standing in front of the locked gates at the park with his arms around a girl, and another of just the girl, flying across the vert ramp.

The city has hired toxicologists to analyze the possible health risks posed by the contaminated water, says Lizbeth DeRocca, director of the Department of Parks and Recreation.

The toxicologists' results should be in within two weeks, but until then, the park remains closed.

"Our preliminary analysis indicates that we're talking about a very low level of contamination," said

DeRocca, "but we're taking every precaution until we know for certain."

The Park Department has posted a guard at the site, after several determined skaters ignored the yellow tape and the warning signs and scaled the fence.

"Skaters aren't always the most law-abiding citizens," says East Bay High student and skating champion C.J. Logan, pictured above with his girlfriend, L Gordon. "They best get that place cleaned up soon if they don't want a massive rebellion on their hands."

Amy looked up. "Just what C.J. Logan's ego needs—not one but *two* pictures of himself in the newspaper. Who's the girl?"

I shrugged. "Never seen her before."

× × ×

All that morning at school, people kept giving me pitying looks or quickly turning to another page in *The Bee* as soon as I came near.

Like Ryan. "Oh, hey, Kelsey," he said, practically jumping out of his seat when I walked by his desk at the beginning of history. He tried to close the copy of

The Bee spread out before him, but I put my hand down on the paper, right smack on the picture of C.J. and L. "Ryan, it's okay."

"But that's . . ."

"C.J. and his new girlfriend. So what?"

"So, didn't you and C.J.—"

"C.J. and I broke up. I'm over him."

"But I heard—"

"Forget what you heard, okay?"

I guess I sounded a little intense, because Ryan held his hands out and said, "Okay. Okay. Chill. I was just trying to, you know, considerate your feelings. Thass all. You don't have to jump all over me."

"Sorry," I said. I plopped myself down into the desk next to him. Then, a little more quietly, I said, "It's just that everyone is treating me like I'm supposed to be in mourning or something, because I'm not with C.J. Logan anymore. And you know what?"

"What?"

"I don't *want* to be with C.J. Logan. *I* broke up with C.J. Logan."

"That's not what I heard," Ryan said, shrugging and looking away. Like I was some poor deluded girl. Too pitiful to look at.

"Ryan, look at me."

He did.

"I broke up with C.J. Logan."

"Okay," he said. But his eyes gave him away. He couldn't keep them on mine.

"You believe me, right?"

"Yeah, Kelsey. I believe you." He blinked three times.

"So I'm fine with this." I pointed to the picture of L skating. "Wow." I hadn't looked at it very closely until then. "She's really good."

Ryan studied the picture. "Yeah. I've never seen a girl do stuff like that."

L was what you would call edgy. In the close-up of her and C.J., I counted four face piercings—eyebrow grommet, lip ring, and two nose rings. But even with all that metal you could tell she was pretty. And of course, she was in excellent, X Game–worthy condition.

She looked wild. And fun. Like if Amy and I just happened to meet her on our own somewhere, we might all three hang out. I wondered what she would do if C.J. trashed her like he did me, which made me wonder if she'd read what he said about me and whether it had bothered her.

x x x

I found Joanna in *The Bee* office at lunch, working on a computer at the back of the room. The girl typed faster than anyone I'd ever seen. I tried to stay calm when I asked her about the story I'd worked on.

"Well, that budget thing just wasn't as dramatic as I thought it was going to be. Sure, there's a trend, but it's not headline material. When that yellow tape went up at the skatepark, I knew we had ourselves a genuine scoop. So I put all my energy into that. It's a *Bee* exclusive. We're the first to break it. *The Chronicle* doesn't have it. *The Tribune* doesn't have it. I'm working on a press release now." She nodded toward her computer monitor. "The TV people are going to be all over this story. The kids who've been using the park might have to get blood tests. Not that that's going to really show anything, 'cause you won't know for ten or twenty years what, if anything, the exposure will do."

"Oh." For the first time, it occurred to me that C.J. wasn't the only one to worry about. Josh had spent a lot of time down there this summer. And what about me? How sad would that be if on top of everything else, being C.J. Logan's Girlfriend gave me cancer? And what about all those little Skater Dudes with their Skater Moms?

"The city's saying it's only a trace amount, not enough to do damage, but . . . Kelsey?"

I looked up. I guess I'd been staring at C.J.'s picture for a while, lost in my worries of future cancer or giving birth to babies with tails. "I hope this isn't too painful for you."

"What?"

She nodded her head toward C.J.'s picture.

"Oh, we've been over for a while."

"Yeah, I heard about that. It sounded really rough. Like you had a hard time letting go. I'm assuming you knew about the new girlfriend already? I'd hate to be responsible for breaking that one to you." She held the paper out to the centerfold.

I shrugged. I hadn't known about the new girlfriend until that morning. But I didn't care about the new girlfriend. At least not in the way people seemed to expect me to. People like Joanna, who was all of a sudden so concerned about my feelings.

"Look, I know you're busy now—"

Joanna looked up from her press release.

"And I know this budget thing wasn't a big deal. But why didn't I get a byline, too?"

"What?" She looked up, as if surprised to find me still there. "Didn't you see the contributor's note?"

"Yeah."

She looked at me for a second and then said, "It's only the actual *writer* who gets the byline. You didn't know that? Researchers get contribution credit. It's standard newspaper practice. It's all spelled out in the handbook."

"Oh." I figured I spent fifteen hours gathering numbers for Joanna's five-hundred-word article about educational spending that she'd probably whipped off in less than an hour.

"But don't worry. We count contributions as half a byline, so it does go into your total for the year."

"Oh."

"Listen, cub."

Did she have to keep calling me that?

"Yeah?"

"I know you're disappointed. And then to have to see your ex-boyfriend on the front page. Plus his new girlfriend." She widened her eyes. "*That's* gotta be tough. I'm sorry about that. You know, your Story Hunt piece might still make it. We're going to be reviewing those over the weekend, and next Monday we'll announce who gets published. Meanwhile, I'm going to keep my eyes out for another story you and I can work on together, okay?"

I didn't know what to say. So I didn't say anything.

I picked up my messenger bag, lifted it over my head, turned around, and left.

"See you seventh period," Joanna said.

Yeah, right. I didn't know if she saw me kick the door shut. And I didn't care.

23

Family Affair

Instead of going to *The Bee* office seventh period, I hung out at the back of the auditorium, watching Amy rehearse for *Footloose*. Theater people are refreshingly oblivious to anyone's gossip but their own tight group's. Nobody even looked at me twice. They were all off in their imaginary small town, somewhere in Oklahoma.

× × ×

When I finally got home that afternoon, I walked in the front door to find Mim, Leonard, and Josh gathered in front of the television.

"They closed the skatepark!" said Josh.

"Did you know about this, Kelsey?" Mim asked.

"Oh, that chemical thing? Yeah, I heard about it."

"I can't believe they would build a park for kids without being more careful." Mim shook her head and held her hand out toward the TV. "I mean, you hear about stuff like this, but you don't think it'll happen where you live."

"This is some seriously toxic stuff they're talking about." Mom's voice came from the kitchen. "Lung cancer, birth defects, sterility, brain damage . . ." She got louder as she named each threat.

I walked back to find her staring at the screen of the kitchen computer.

"Mom, that's only if you're, like, drinking the stuff."

The look in her eye told me it was too late. She was in full hazard-mongering mode. She grabbed the phone next to her. "I'm calling Ed Logan."

Gulp. Ed Logan was C.J.'s neurologist-father.

"He'll know if this is something we need to be concerned about. What's their number?"

"Umm . . . I deleted it from my cell." Actually, I hadn't gotten around to erasing all of C.J.'s numbers, but I had every intention of doing so, and I had no intention of aiding and abetting a conversation between his father and my mother.

Mom had no idea. Mom and I are pretty open, but I just wasn't ready to share that one. I mean, what was I supposed to say, "Um, Mom, C.J. wrote about our really hot not-quite-sex life on the Internet"? Plus, knowing my mother, if she had known, she probably would have called C.J.'s parents or threatened to sue him or something like that, which wouldn't exactly help me in the reputation department.

"There's C.J.!" Josh yelled from the living room. "You guys, come here. Quick!"

Mom and I ran into the living room.

"Turn it up, Josh," said Mim.

Josh blasted the volume just as a perky blonde reporter said, "Thanks, Ken. We're here live at the Berkeley skatepark with C.J. Logan, a young man whose name is synonymous with skateboarding in Northern California.

"C.J., you've been skating at this park since it opened two years ago. Tell us, aren't you concerned about the discovery of hexavalent chromium in the groundwater?"

C.J. shrugged and looked over his shoulder to the locked fence behind him. "Only 'cause now we don't have anywhere to skate."

"You're not concerned about the health hazards? Experts say this chemical has been known to cause cancer, brain damage—"

C.J. smiled. "Doesn't sound much more dangerous than skating. Look, it's nice they're looking out for us and all . . . but, I mean, there's, like, two feet of concrete between us and the ground. We'd be out there skating right now if you all weren't here with your cameras. And if that dude wasn't over there makin' sure we don't climb the fence." C.J. smiled and waved at someone off to the side. The camera panned over to a uniformed cop, complete with mirrored sunglasses, standing in front of the locked gate. He waved—but didn't smile—back at C.J. Between C.J. and the cop stood the whole skating crowd. Flip and S-man, and I was pretty sure I saw L, the new girlfriend.

My whole family laughed. "That C.J.," said Mim, with an appreciative, grandmotherly head shake. If she only knew.

Meanwhile, Mom had gotten the phone book out and was flipping through the pages. "Logan . . . Logan . . . Here it is." She punched in the number before I could think of any way to stop her. "Hello Jen? Barbara Wilcox here, Kelsey's mother?"

. . .

"Hi, how *are* you?"

. . .

"Uh-huh . . . Uh-huh . . ." Mom put her hand over the phone.

"Does she always go on like this?" C.J.'s mom was quite a talker. All you had to do was ask her one question and she'd be going for fifteen minutes. "Listen, Jen, I'm sorry to interrupt, but the reason I'm calling is to find out what you guys know about this chemical they found at the skatepark."

. . .

"Yeah. Kelsey thinks I'm overreacting. So what does Ed think? Is this something I need to worry about?"

. . .

"Oh?"

. . .

"Oh?"

. . .

"Really? Okay, well then, if Ed's not worried, then I won't be, either. But they'd better get that stuff cleaned up, and they'd better hope that none of those kids comes down with anything mysterious over the next five years. Okay, thanks a lot."

. . .

"Yeah." Mom glanced my way. "I know, it is too bad. But they're so young." Mom looked at me again. This time quizzically. "Oh she's fine."

. . .

"Yes, really. Fine." Mom shrugged at me. "In fact, she started writing for the paper this year. . . . And C.J.? He looked great on the news. He always looks great."

. . .

"Oh?"

. . .

"Uh-huh."

. . .

"Sounds great. Listen, thanks a lot, Jen. I'm glad I thought to call you. It's such a relief. Give my best to Ed. And to C.J., too."

Mom hung up and took a deep breath.

"They're not worried?" asked Mim.

"Nope." Mom shook her head. "Jen said Ed said what Kelsey said: If they weren't drinking it, there really isn't anything to worry about. It's possible that some got absorbed into the concrete, but not enough to do any harm."

"Oh, that's such a relief," Mim said, holding her hand to her heart. "For a while there I thought I might not get those great-grandchildren I was planning to live long enough to know."

"That was a strange call, though," Mom said,

looking at me. "Jen seemed very concerned about Kelsey's spirits. She asked if you were 'doing better than in the summer.' "

"Really?" I said, trying to sound natural and surprised but sounding high-pitched and weird.

"Yeah. From the way she was talking, it sounded like she thought you'd been through a terrible heartbreak. Like I should have had you on suicide watch. Didn't you tell us it was a mutual decision, Kels?"

"Yup. It was." I'd given my family the old "we just grew apart" story, saying that C.J.'s skating was taking up all his time, and that we'd arrived at "a mutual agreement." I thought it would keep them from asking questions. And until now, it had.

Josh, who had been flipping back and forth between the other local news channels, looked at me for a long second, then back to the TV, then at me again, and back to the TV again. Something about the way he looked at me told me he knew. That he must have read C.J.'s lies about me.

Mom noticed and said, "What?"

"Nothing," I said, looking at Josh, who pretended to be concentrating on his channel-flipping.

"Did I miss something? You guys went out of town the morning after you broke up, and you seemed fine then. Your dad said you had a great time, that you seemed happy. Should I have been paying more attention?"

"Mom, I was fine. I am fine. I told you, it was a mutual thing. I don't even think about C.J. anymore." Which wasn't exactly true. But true enough for the purposes of this conversation. I wasn't pining or anything.

Josh looked at me again. Was it possible that he actually believed the stuff C.J. wrote?

Thank God Mom's cell phone rang just then, and she went back to the kitchen to talk to someone from the *Law Review* about some deadline. If I was lucky, she'd get all caught up in whatever emergency was happening there and forget about this unfinished conversation.

x x x

"Josh?"

"Yeah?" His eyes didn't budge from the video game he'd turned on after the news.

"Why did you look at me like that?"

"Like what?

"Funny. You looked at me funny."

He turned to me. "No, I didn't." He was blushing, and having trouble meeting my eyes.

"Yeah, you did. Did you read C.J.'s blog after we broke up?"

He sent his animated duck on a motorcycle zooming across the screen, knocking over whatever was in its way. "What blog?"

"Josh, I think you know what I'm talking about. The stuff C.J. wrote . . . about . . . our breakup."

Josh was silent. The motorcycle slammed into a bus.

"And about me."

He shrugged unconvincingly and started a new game. "I don't know what you're talking about."

"Well, it's all a lie, by the way. C.J. made it all up."

"Oh."

"I actually broke up with him."

Another shrug. The motorcycling duck zoomed across an old lady's garden. "Whatever."

"It's true."

Josh finally turned away from the screen and met my eyes. "Yeah, well, thanks for ruining my life." He turned back to his game.

"Excuse me? Ruining *your* life?"

"Yeah. C.J. doesn't even say 'Hey' to me anymore thanks to you—"

"Josh—"

"What?" Yeah, what? What exactly am I supposed to say to my ten-year-old brother who thinks I might be a slut—a desperate, stalking slut?

"Never mind." This had gone on long enough.

I'd lived with this thing for weeks. I had endured a very long day of pitying looks and snickers, and I might have been able to go on like that. But the thought of my little brother reading and believing that crap—or thinking that it was okay to talk about girls like that—made me madder than I could ever remember being. Something had to be done.

If I worked fast enough, I might still catch C.J. at the skatepark.

But there was one thing I had to do first. I ran up to my room and turned on my computer.

24

F 2 F

A few minutes later, I found Mim back in her office, standing in front of her file cabinet with the drawer out and a pile of files on top.

"Um, Mim?"

"Yes, honey?"

"I need you to drive me somewhere. And I need you not to ask me questions about it."

"Okay . . . I guess." She rolled the file drawer in. "Am I allowed to ask where?"

"To the skatepark. I've got to talk to C.J. And I'm sorry, but that's all I'm telling you. Trust me, I wouldn't ask if it wasn't absolutely necessary at this minute for you to take me there."

"Oh, honey, are you sure this is a good idea? Have you thought about writing your feelings down?

Some of my clients find that can be helpful."

"Mim, this is something I have to do. And I have to do it face-to-face. I've already waited too long. So could you just—trust me? And help me?"

"Yes. Of course I will."

× × ×

When Mim's Volvo pulled up to the curb next to the park entrance, a news van was packing up, and a bunch of kids were milling around on the sidewalk.

"I'll get out here. I won't be long." Mim reached over and squeezed my arm as I opened the car door and got out.

C.J.'s dog, Trippy, was the first to notice me. He bolted over all waggedy-tailed and jumped on my leg. Julie Miller whispered something to Kiki Alteri, who turned to look at me, smirked, and whispered something to her boyfriend, Flip, who was standing between her and C.J. Kiki and Flip stepped to the side and there was C.J., standing at the center of the group, wrapped around the girl I recognized as L. He had one hand in her back pocket. His other arm was slung across her shoulder and tucked into her waist.

Exactly how he used to hold me.

When C.J. first saw me, he smiled. Like how he did way back when we were just getting to know each other. And then, in a split second, the smile vanished.

"Hey, Kelsey." C.J. lifted his chin. "Too late to get on TV, the cameras are all gone." He laughed at his own joke and looked around at the others. Flip and S-Man chuckled and their girls sneered. L smiled and looked at me.

I didn't say anything to C.J. Instead, I looked L in the eye and said, "Hi. You must be L." She looked up at C.J., who had stopped smiling, and then back at me.

"Yeah?"

"I'm the previous girlfriend. You may have heard of me—"

She tilted her head up at C.J. He looked nervous.

"Kelsey," said L with a slow nod.

"Yup, that's me, a.k.a. the TSF." I offered my hand.

She stared at it. "TS—?" From the look on her face, it seemed L had no idea what I was talking about.

"Hey, Kelsey. Come on." C.J. lifted the hand that was tucked into L's waist and held it out in front of her, like she needed protection. From me.

I went right on talking to L.

"That's a killer move," I said, tilting my head toward C.J.'s other hand. "Isn't it? The hand in the back pocket, I mean. And when he whispers in your ear. No resisting that one. Does he pull on your hair?" I ran my eyes down her long, black hair. "That's when I lost it."

C.J. let go of L completely and stepped between her and me. "Come on, Kelsey. What are you doing?"

I pulled the paper out of my front pocket and unfolded it. Before talking to Mim, I'd printed out the stuff about me from C.J.'s blog. At the time, I wasn't exactly sure what I was going to do with it. I still wasn't exactly sure what I was doing. Instinct had taken over. And it felt right.

"I'm doing what I should have done a long time ago, C.J." I poked my head over his shoulder and said to L, "Look, I'm really sorry to intrude here. I'll be gone in a second. My grandmother's waiting for me in that old Volvo over there."

Everybody looked toward Mim's car. She rolled down her window, stuck her head out, and waved. What exactly did she think was going on over here?

C.J. waved back, and turned to me.

"Don't worry, they still think you're a nice guy."

I held the paper out to C.J. "Do you want to read this, or should I?"

He glanced down and recognized his TSF rant. He shook his head. "Kelsey . . ."

"I want to know if you have the guts to read your words out loud. To my face."

He just stood there, staring at the paper.

"That's what I thought. Okay. I'll read it. It's not like there's anyone here who hasn't read it for themselves. Except maybe my replacement over there. Ahem, 'To all y'all who keep buggin me: Yeah, we broke up. Had to happen. The girl's a Total—' "

"Kelsey, come on, that's in the past. Let's just leave it there and . . . and move on."

" 'In the past'? In the past, C.J.? No it's not in the past. Not in *my* past. Not in *our* past. This," I said, holding the paper up, "exists only in your head." I paused. "Oh yeah, and on the Internet, where anyone—including my ten-year-old brother—can read it."

"Kelsey, come here." C.J. took a few steps down the sidewalk, apparently expecting me to follow. "Let's talk in private."

"Hah." I turned toward him but didn't budge. "*Now* you want to talk in private? When it's your reputation, we have to keep it on the QT. But mine you can blast to shreds all over cyberspace."

"Kelsey—I'm sorry."

"Now we're getting somewhere. Go on. You're sorry?"

He walked back, so that he was standing right in front of me. "Yeah." He glanced at L, who was watching with her arms folded in front of her. "I'm sorry things didn't work out."

"Nuh-uh. Sorry, but *that* sorry won't do." I raised my voice a notch. "Let's see, where was I? Oh yeah. 'The girl's a Total . . . Sex Fiend. Never wanted to do anything else. I mean, come on, it's usually the girls who complain that we have only one thing on our minds . . .' "

"I'm sorry—"

"Yes, C.J.?"

I followed his eyes over to L. She'd put her skateboard down on the sidewalk and had one foot on it, like she was ready to roll away.

"L, don't . . ." She pushed off. C.J. turned to me. "Great, now look what you did."

"What *I* did? You amaze me, C.J., you really do."

He put his hands on his hips and looked over at Flip and S-Man, who were both studying the sidewalk in front of them. Julie and Kiki were whispering to each other.

" 'She cried when I told her. Which almost got to me . . .'" I paused for effect, and put my hand over my heart. " . . . but I was strong.' "

"Okay, okay. Stop."

"Stop?"

"Please?" He turned and yelled, "L, wait up!" But she kept on rolling. He turned back to me. "I'll delete it. All of it. Tonight. As soon as I get home."

"Okayyyy, that's a start."

"What else do you want from me? You probably just lost me my new girlfriend, too. Isn't that enough?"

I shook my head. "You know what I want."

He looked at the ground, then down the sidewalk. L had disappeared.

"Okay. I'm sorry. How's that?"

"That's good. That's good, C.J. But not good enough. You're sorry for what, exactly?"

Looking at the ground, he said, "I'm sorry—" He shifted his feet and put his hands in his pockets. "I'm sorry I—" Then, for the first time since the last time we sat in his pickup together, C.J. looked me in the eye. "I'm sorry I made that stuff up about you. I'm sorry, Kelsey."

"Thank you." I turned and walked away as he jogged down the sidewalk in futile pursuit of the second girl in history to dump C.J. Logan.

25

Dignity

It's amazing what standing up for herself—live and in person—can do for a girl's mood.

When I went back to school the next day, I felt good. Better, even, than I'd felt the whole year before, when I had that girlfriend-of-a-celebrity glow. Way better.

I walked up the steps and in the front door, without worrying about who might be there to give me what kind of look. When I crossed the courtyard to meet Amy for lunch, I felt like I actually *was* flying. I'd been walking around for so long carrying the weight of C.J.'s lies. Without it, I felt incredibly light.

C.J.'s crew was in their usual spot that day, but C.J. was missing. I didn't see him the day after, or the day after that. Eventually, after a week or so, he showed up again. Right there at the center of the circle. Whatever damage his reputation had suffered from our little showdown didn't last. He was, after all, still C.J. Logan, master of the vert ramp, the dude who'd been on the cover of *Thrasher* (twice), the dude everyone wanted to know.

Everyone except me. And Amy. And L, who wrote me a few e-mails after the Big Showdown. She's the one who told me that C.J. found himself a new girlfriend not so long after L escaped. One of the Fan Club Girls, "guaranteed not to dump him," was how she put it.

So not a lot changed for C.J. after the Big Showdown.

But a lot changed for me.

Now, I could tell you that calling C.J. out on his lies freed me forever from the burden of caring about what people think of me or say about me. But, really, is there anyone on earth—other than Mim and the Dalai Lama—who's *that* free?

The Big Showdown left me caring a lot less, though.

And when I walked back into *The Bee* office on the day they were announcing the fate of our Story Hunt entries—which was the first time I saw Nathan since he ran away from me in the basement of the

Board of Ed building—I can truly say I was more focused on whether my story was going to make it into the paper than I was on what Nathan thought of me. It was close. But the professional definitely outweighed the personal.

When I had stomped out of *The Bee* office on the day Joanna put C.J. on the cover, I thought I'd never go back. But facing C.J. helped clarify things for me. I realized I really wanted to write for *The Bee*. That it wasn't just about finding some new way to identify myself now that I was no longer C.J. Logan's Girlfriend. Yeah, Joanna was a pain, but I could deal with it. I liked my article about Star. I was totally scared that day when I met her, but I liked the challenge of getting her to talk to me. And then trying to understand what her life was like, and then trying to write about that life in a way that would matter to the other kids at school. However "chatty" my article was, I thought people would want to read it.

And so I went back to *The Bee*, and I looked Joanna right in the eye and said "Hey" when I walked in. She didn't exactly smile and welcome me with open arms. But she didn't scowl either when she said "Hey" back.

I sat down next to Ryan, who had high hopes for the article he'd submitted. He was acting all smug and refusing to tell anyone what it was about.

Nathan walked in at the very last minute, just as the bell ran. He dug his clipboard out of his bag and walked to the front of the room. When he saw me, he raised his eyebrows and lifted his chin. I blushed.

"Okay, cubs. First of all, I want—" Joanna cleared her throat. Nathan looked at her, smiled apologetically, and said, "*We* would like to thank everyone for their hard work on their Story Hunt pieces. We've got a lot of new talent and energy in this room, and I think it's safe to say that *The Bee* tradition of excellence in high-school journalism will continue after Jo and I are gone."

Next it was Joanna's turn. "Now, I'm about to read a list of reporters whose articles will be published in the next issue. If you don't hear your name"—I'm still not sure if it was my imagination or if she really looked at me when she said that—"don't be disappointed. It's going to be a long school year, and we'll have lots of stories that need covering." Uh-oh.

"Okay, now, without further ado"—she cleared her throat, which to me qualified as further ado—"cub reporters whose work will appear in the next *Bee* are: Mona Nadell . . ." Joanna nodded toward Mona, who was sitting in front of her. "Mona did an excellent job surveying the faculty on the new state exit exam, which we are all going to have to take to get out of this place. Let's hear it for Mona."

We all clapped.

"Next." While Joanna went down her list, I could sense Nathan looking at me. But when I looked at him, he looked away. "Next, we have an unusual story. A piece that shows a great deal of initiative and imagination. . . ." Joanna paused and looked around the room. Turning to Ryan, she said, "Mr. Ryan Stansfield got himself a ride-along after all. And he's got the pictures to prove it. . . ." Ryan smiled as he held up a picture of himself hanging off the side of a garbage truck, wearing a yellow jumpsuit, heavy work gloves, and a thick back-protecting belt. "Ryan," said Joanna, "spent a whole morning with the sanitation workers, and he wrote a kick-ass piece about how much recyclable stuff gets thrown in the trash. Let's hear it for Ryan."

While everyone clapped, Ryan stood up and took a bow.

Joanna read off two more names. Roxanna Johnson, who wrote about the problem of the leaky roof on the girls' locker room, for which there was no repair money available, and Elijah Summers Tucker, who went undercover as a person looking for an aura reading from the Psychic Institute up the street from our school.

"With these stories, the next *Bee* is going to be a 'must-read.'" Joanna dropped her clipboard to her side.

So much for my new, post-C.J. good mood. Ryan leaned over to my desk. "You was robbed, girl. That article you wrote had style."

I shrugged. "I guess it was too 'chatty.'" I looked over at Nathan, who was staring at Joanna and about to speak.

"Umm . . . Jo?"

"Yeah?"

"Didn't you forget one?"

"Did I?" She looked at her clipboard for a couple seconds. Then, without lifting her eyes from her clipboard, she said, "Oh, yeah," like it was some minor detail she'd overlooked. "And Kelsey Wilcox's 'Her Name Is Star' will appear on the Op-Ed page, along with her photographs."

× × ×

A few days later, I found "Her Name Is Star" taped to my locker. Someone had circled my byline in shiny silver ink and attached a giant purple-and-silver balloon with Bart Simpson on it saying, "Congratulations, Dude."

At first I assumed it was Amy. But when I turned over the card attached to the balloon's ribbon, I read, "Great job, cub! Congratulations on your first byline. Your Editors."

For a second I wondered if it was Amy's idea of a joke. But her handwriting is loopy and the card was written in straight, bold print. So straight and bold that, at first, I thought it had been typed. But "Great" and "job" had been underlined with jaggedy lines you could see had been made with a ballpoint. While I stood there studying the card, Nathan walked up.

"Hey . . . congratulations."

"Thanks—and thanks for this, I guess?" I yanked on the ribbon, and Bart did a little helium jig in the air.

"It's not every day you get your first byline." He yanked on the ribbon, too.

"But you guys didn't have to—"

"Yeah we did. It's a *Bee* tradition. See?" He pointed down the hall to where Ryan stood in front of his locker, another Bart balloon bobbing above his head. "Actually, Joanna's the one who started the balloons. In the past they just taped the article."

"Joanna did?"

"Yeah. Don't look so surprised. She's actually a nice person when she isn't—" Nathan looked down at his shoes. One of the laces was untied, and I blushed as I remembered tying his shoes in the closet that day.

"Out-of-her-mind stressed?" I offered.

"Yeah. And she really does care about *The Bee* and carrying on all the traditions."

"I get the distinct impression she wouldn't mind very much if those traditions went on without me."

"Oh, she's just . . . It's just . . ." Nathan shifted his feet and ran a hand through his hair. "She thinks . . . She's got it in her head that there's something going on between you and me."

I laughed. A high-pitched totally geeky-sounding laugh.

"Which, I told her, is highly unlikely. . . ."

I nodded. "Highly."

"'Cause I'm not about to—"

"Yeah. Me neither."

"There's just too much going on—"

"Yeah." Like Miss Italy, for example?

"It's hard after so much time. It's weird, too, because at first she was the one who wanted to end things."

"She was?"

"Yeah. We really bit it junior year. Fought all the time. She said she didn't want us to be one of those couples that hangs on just so they can say they made it all the way through high school."

"But—"

"What?"

"I thought—" Did I want to tell Nathan that I'd spent time thinking about his and Joanna's relationship?

"Don't tell me you heard that crap about the e-mail? And the Swiss princess?"

"Italian. I heard it was an Italian contessa."

Nathan shook his head and rolled his eyes.

"Joanna and I broke up at the beginning of the summer. It was totally mutual, but like I said, she was the one to initiate. I went to Europe on this backpacking trip. After a couple weeks out in the boonies, we finally got to an Internet café. So I log on, and what do I find but all these e-mails from her saying she thinks we made a mistake. Maybe we should just stick it out through graduation. But by then . . ." He looked at me. "Well, I was liking being on my own. Making new friends. She was Swiss—French Swiss—and there was some old aristocratic somebody in her family tree, but she was just a girl, you know? A high-school girl, and it wasn't really anything but a little summer, you know, friendship kind of fun thing. . . . And she wasn't the *reason* I told Joanna I thought it was really for the best. Then I come back to find out that half the senior class—the female half—thinks I'm a jerk because I supposedly blew my girlfriend of three years off with an e-mail."

Nathan looked directly at me. "Please don't tell me you believed that, too."

I shrugged.

"You of all people should know better than to believe what you hear."

I blushed. "Yeah. I guess I should."

The bell rang. Nathan untied Bart's ribbon from my locker and held it out for me. "So. Congratulations, cub."

I curled my fingers around the ribbon. "Thanks."

"See you this afternoon?"

"Yeah."

"And again on Wednesday afternoon?"

"Yeah. . . ."

"And then again next Monday?" Nathan smiled.

I smiled back. "Yup."

"Good."

× × ×

All over school that day, I watched as people read my article and looked at my pictures. Part of me was, as they say, bursting with pride. I wanted to shout, "Hey, I wrote that! That picture? Mine. Snapped it just in time." But this other part of me, the better part, didn't care about getting credit. I just wanted to watch as people read about Star and what she'd been through. For the time it took them to read my words and look at my pictures, people were paying attention—thinking about her life on the street and what made her supposedly "choose" that life.

Of course I knew that my little story wasn't exactly going to solve the homeless youth problem or anything. But maybe some of the people who read my story wouldn't be so quick to scurry by Star or her friends next time they were shopping on Telegraph. Maybe they'd make eye contact and say hi, or stop to pet Max and ask Star something about herself.

I would, at least.

Two Months Later

The room smelled like cold cream and sweat.

Three girls sat in front of the brightly lit mirror. Each wore a uniquely arty robe. Amy's was the tackiest thing I'd ever seen: turquoise terry cloth with an orange zipper, and bright orange and fuchsia birds embroidered on the collar. She'd been thrilled to find it at Sal's vintage store the week before.

"This is perfect for backstage. It's perfect!"

Did you ever notice how theater people are always in costume, even when they're backstage, supposedly changing back into themselves?

I approached from the side, so Amy couldn't see me in the mirror. "Surprise!" I placed the flowers, which I had spent an hour at the store picking out and arranging, in her lap. "You were great! Amazing. Fabulous."

It was opening night of *Footloose* and Amy had been great, amazing, and fabulous.

She picked up the bouquet and stood up to hug me. "Thanks, best friend. I wonder what my mother thought."

"I would say that even if I were your worst enemy, I swear, when you walked onto that stage tonight, you lit the whole place up."

"That was Danny, the light man."

"Ha. Seriously, it was more than that."

Amy played Urleen, one of the three friends of the female lead, Ariel, who, according to tradition, was played by a graduating senior. I was sure that if it weren't for that rule, Amy would have nailed the lead. She is that good.

And she's amazingly professional, too. One of the other two best friends, Rusty, was played by none other than Giselle, the girl Gabe dumped Amy for. I guess Giselle was a pretty good actress, too, because you would never know, from the way they were onstage, that they hated each other in real life. Amy said they'd gotten through the whole rehearsal period without uttering a single word to each other except for their lines.

"You totally stood out." I said that for Giselle's benefit. She was sitting at the other end of the bench, in a pink sheer dressing gown with a faux-fur trim. If she heard me, she didn't let on. She went right on running a Q-Tip around her kohl-ringed eyes.

"So . . . to the Hut for a celebratory opening-night mocha? Just us?"

"But what about . . . ?"

"I told him another time. This is your night."